T0117545

OH, DON'T ASK WHY

OH, DON'T ASK WHY

STORIES

DENNIS MUST

...

RED HEN PRESS | *Pasadena, CA*

Oh, Don't Ask Why
Copyright © 2017, 2007 by Dennis Must
All Rights Reserved

Book design by Mark E. Cull

ISBN: 978-1-59709-033-9
Library of Congress Control Number: 2005932929

The National Endowment for the Arts, the Los Angeles County Arts
Commission, the Dwight Stuart Youth Fund, the Max Factor Family
Foundation, the Pasadena Tournament of Roses Foundation, the Pasa-
dena Arts & Culture Commission and the City of Pasadena Cultural
Affairs Division, the City of Los Angeles Department of Cultural Af-
fairs, the Audrey & Sydney Irmas Charitable Foundation, Sony Pictures
Entertainment, Amazon Literary Partnership, and the Sherwood Foun-
dation partially support Red Hen Press.

Second Edition
Published by Red Hen Press
www.redhen.org

ACKNOWLEDGMENTS

The author gratefully acknowledges the publishers of periodicals in which these stories first appeared:

"Typewriter": *Portland Review*, Portland State University, Portland OR, 2000; *elimae*, 2001, *Green Hills Literary Lantern*, Truman State University, MO, 2002, *Terrain*, 2003, "Grief": *Exquisite Corpse*, 2000; "The Hireling": *Full Circle, A Journal of Poetry and Prose*, 2003; "Queen Esther": *Red Cedar Review*, Michigan State University, 2000, *Aura Literary/Arts Review*, University of Alabama, 2000, *The Able Muse*, 2000; "The Avengers": *CrossConnect*, University of Pennsylvania, April 2003; "Tracks": *Conspire*, 1999; "The Rooming House": *RE:AL*, SFA State University, TX, 2000, *Southern Ocean Review*, 2000; "Mechanic": *Amarillo Bay*, 1999; *Princeton Arts Review, 1999, Eclectica Magazine*, 1999; "Scatology": *Big Bridge*, 1999; "The News From Heaven": *Readers Break Anthology*, 1999; *Avatar Review*, 2000; SOIL: *Savoy Magazine*, 1999; "Ambush": *Orange Willow Review*, 1998; *Terrain*, 2000; "Portmanteau": *elimae*, 2001; "Star-Crossed": *Bayou*, University of New Orleans, 2002; *The Wag*, 2003; "Combustion": *Exquisite Corpse*, 2001; *Unlikely Stories*, 2001; "Lament": *Linnaean Street*, 2001; *LIT Magazine, New School University*, 2005; "She's A Little Store Inside": *The Baltimore Review*, 2003; GSU Review, Georgia State University, 2003; Lullwater Review, Emory University, GA, 2003; *elimae*, 2004; "The Bandoneon": *Main Street Rag*, Charlotte, NC, 2004; "Circus Man": *pacific REVIEW*, San Diego State University, 2003; "I Think Jesus Is Fred Astaire": *VerbSap*, 2005; "St. James Hotel": *Snow Monkey*, 2006

For my daughters
Kim, Kathy, Shawn, Shoshanna, Ariel

CONTENTS

Oh, show us the way
To the next whisky-bar!
Oh, don't ask why; oh don't ask why!

Alabama-Song
—Weill/Brecht

TYPEWRITER

The room had one window, a metal cot, a lime-green chest of draw-ers, and a mirror that hung on the backside of its shellacked door. The distance between the bureau and the bed was the width of a heavyset man. Twelve pairs of shoes placed toe to heel its length.

Each morning an attendant in a cotton electric-blue uniform knocked. Did he want his bed made?

Muller always said no.

A portable Royal typewriter sat on the bureau alongside a comb and a straight razor. Tenants stole each other's rations. Over the weeks of his stay he cinched his belt tighter, taking insidious plea-sure in returning to the weight he held as a young man. On his trips to the Single Room Occupancy's bathroom he'd open the bare communal refrigerator and laugh to himself. A second mirror.

It'd been one week since the trace of onion juice and ground meat had all but disappeared from his clothes. But so had most of the wages he'd earned on the grill. When hunger began to threaten his concentration, he'd lie down upon the cot, look up at the cracked ceiling, and visualize lemon meringue pie—the White Tower spe-cialty. Methodically he'd cut himself a wedge, then, savoring each bite, even the ceiling crumbs, he'd devour the memory.

The lunch surfeit would carry him to the evening meal at Horn & Hardart. These latter days it consisted of a serving of Parker

House Rolls and a glass of milk. Packets of sugar cubes he'd pocket to melt in a hot-water drink for bedtime.

Muller had no clock. The thread from morning to half-light or darkness was the clacking of his typewriter. After dressing and splashing cold water on his face each dawn, he'd lift the instrument off the bureau, pull the window blind down so that the room was in virtual blackness, and sit on the bed to begin working with his back against the wall.

He typed for hours, interrupted only by the ceiling repast. When his output was niggardly, he'd punish himself.

"I can't look at the pastry," he'd cry, staring vacantly into the darkness. Even the sugar tea was off limits.

Muller had no idea what he was writing, for that was the presumption. "If I know what I'm about to compose, then what is its value?" Better to absent oneself as the machine clacked, one page of text followed by another, all hammered onto the white rice paper in darkness. Prior to turning in each night he'd gather the pages in sequence and resist reading them under the overhead light.

Actually there was somebody else inside his room.

A genius of a writer, Muller believed—for whom he was the designated medium.

"Talk to me," he'd urge. "I'll get it all down."

In the early days of their tenancy it would take hours for the guest to break his reticence. As noontime approached—bodies shuffled in the hallway, a sign they were traveling to the empty refrigerator—Muller grew increasingly anxious. The Riverside Suites tenants passing his door mid-afternoon could hear him utter "Please."

But at other times they'd hear him instruct: "Don't palaver to me. No, I'm not listening. Yes, I am getting it all down. *Get to the good stuff, please!*"

The 7th floor residents had no way of knowing, however, that the intervals of absolute daylight behind tenancy 65 signaled that its two occupants were dining on ceiling pie.

"The more I encourage him to speak, the greater the chance that he will utter a story never before spoken. My manuscript's pages will be rife with layered meaning, more than I could ever cause to come out of my brain—that weak handmaiden of reason." And as the September days progressed, the hallway travelers were now accustomed to hearing one voice pleading: "Please, I'm hungry. Can we eat the pie?"

Sternly rebuked by, "More words. Another ten minutes of words, then we'll break."

The Royal literally clacked away from morning to evening with scarce snacking periods—or toilet calls—in between. Days earlier the housekeeper had given up on knocking on Room 65's door.

Muller now slept wearing his clothes on top of a bare mattress.

Each morning before placing the typewriter on his lap, he'd hold the growing sheath of papers in his right hand, and fan them with his left. "Soon it will all be worth it," he'd reflect. Even his belt was now two sizes too large. An occasional giddiness had begun to set in.

His opening of the empty refrigerator at the end of the corridor now provoked bald laughter. And four days before the close of the two-week period, Muller made a decision: "The voice—I can't shut him up at night. I mustn't sleep."

On Saturday the management would escort him out to the street.

"We've only three days left," he cautioned his guest. "Finish up. I must return home to resume my duties as father and loving husband. Complete your tale, I beg of you."

The hallway denizens no longer heard cries for "More lemon meringue, please!", merely the furious clacking of the metal typewriter keys against the hard rubber roller. Inside his cell Muller didn't even look up at the ceiling. Sugar cubes lay unopened in their Horn & Hardart wrappers.

And he mocked the sad refrigerator without remorse.

Like a court reporter's, Muller's fingers, the final twenty-four hours, blazed over the Royal's keyboard. He'd decipher his guest's narrative once he was done. Further, whoever was so privileged to record a disembodied voice willing to reveal its secrets, to spin its narrative untrammeled? Ernest Muller, the happy medium, tapping it all out furiously for posterity.

Saturday morning, on the fourteenth day, he ceased typing. The sun had just begun to cut across his wall. The assembled manuscript, two inches thick, sat at his side. Mysterious its contents. Even up to the last hour Muller sensed there was so much more his guest wanted to say. That he, Muller, understood in the latter days of the testimony the pair was repelling down deeper caverns. If only he could hold out, the manuscript would become even richer.

That, in fact, he might not ever again have to eat, or waste long hours sleeping. His typing now so regular in rhythm it beat loudly like the heart he no longer heard.

But Muller also knew that any moment a key would be placed into his door's lock. There were only several coins on the bureau's top. It was time to throw water on his face, mock the Frigidaire one last time, and descend the SRO's stairs to the brisk October air—his manuscript wrapped tightly against his person.

Outside, the street's shop windows moved in and out of focus. He was having difficulty moving forward.

"I must adjust," he thought. "The light is blinding me. I have to be stronger."

He clung tighter to the manuscript. "How do I get back home to Pittsburgh?" he worried. "I've seventy-eight cents to my name." Purposely Muller had made no friends in Gotham so that, uninterrupted, he could complete the manuscript. "Now that I've accomplished that, I must concentrate on getting back to the life I've left behind. *But will they still be there?*" he fretted. Was Grace still waiting for him? And what if she wasn't? How could he work if he was unable to walk straight and continued to be seduced by the guest's narrative?

Get it down, Muller, make sure you get it all down.

The manuscript felt extra heavy.

"I must get back home."

He approached a blood bank storefront. *"Seven dollars for the first pint. Twelve dollars for each successive pint,"* a placard in the window advertised.

"I've two units to donate," Muller told the receptionist.

In a thick German accent, a white-smocked attendant replied, "Today we take one pint. Fourteen days, you return—we take another. *Then* give you twelve dollars for the second."

Muller lay upon the metal table and stared at the ceiling.

"Clench a fist and pump it!" the attendant ordered after inserting the needle in Muller's forearm. Several bodies on either side of him, all vagrants, opening and closing their fists as the blood spurted into plastic pouches suspended like vermilion bats from chromium rods.

At some point in the bloodletting procedure, Muller heard his guest's voice:

"Hurry! Get to the typewriter. I've much more to tell you."

"But I've no typewriter!" he cried.

"It's here sitting on the cot. We're waiting for you," the guest assured, lamenting, *"The unexamined life is not worth living.* Furthermore, I'm famished."

Muller twisted and turned on the gurney, awaking to the foreign doctor bending solicitously over him. "You should not be giving your blood." They drew the needle out of his arm.

"I must have the money!" Muller cried.

The doctor instructed the attendant to remove seven dollars out of the cash register.

"But, sir . . ." The donor's pouch was half full.

"It's all he can afford." The physician said, placing the bills into Muller's hand. "Nobody in Babylon will pick you up if you collapse on its streets." He studied the manuscript still firmly gripped to Muller's side. "It is valuable, no?" Muller nodded. "Then for its sake and yours—get something to eat, now."

A window poster across the street displayed a Salisbury steak with mashed potatoes and gravy; two pats of butter melted on a side of sliced carrots. A Woolworth five-dollar special that included a beverage of choice.

Muller spent his blood money on dinner, then placed a call to his wife.

"Hi, this is Ernest. I'm ready to come home."

He heard a heavy sigh.

"Grace?"

"Muller, why do you want to come home?" her weary response.

"Because of you and Laurel."

"Where are you calling from anyway?"

"New York City."

"You making it big like you said you could?"

A sliver of sarcasm in her voice. It hadn't started out that way. But now these were the only two people in the whole world who were legally attached to him. And if she didn't want him . . .

"Please stay there, Ernest. Laurel and me—when she grows up and you become famous—then I'll tell her about her daddy. It's peaceful here since you left. I've put up new curtains. And painted our bathroom canary yellow."

"Grace, I want to come home."

Would she break down and say OK? If I can just get her to wire me bus fare. "I'll make it right for you and the child, I promise. I'll get a job like other fathers. I'll buy a suit and a hat and earn a respectable wage.

"I've been doing much thinking of late since I've been alone. I'm not the same person. In fact I'm even a short order cook. When I get back I'll fry eggs in our black skillet the Big Whitey way."

Her voice was bone dry. "What is it you want from us, Ernest?"

"Twenty dollars."

Grace dropped the phone. He could see the receiver swinging pendulum-like on the kitchen wall as she shuffled off in her felt slippers, looking for a pencil.

Muller walked to the nearby Western Union Office and sat on its bench waiting until the next morning, when at 11:05 the clerk handed him the cash.

"Was there any message?" he asked.

The clerk shook his head, grinning. "There would have been, mister, if the dough hadn't arrived—huh?"

That afternoon somewhere between the Hershey and Breeze-wood Pennsylvania turnpike exchanges Muller chanced a look at the manuscript. It sat alongside him in the rear of the fume-laden Greyhound bus. With a blend of excitement and dread he pealed the last thirty pages off the packet, and began reading.

Within seconds he grew pale and began trembling.

The Frigidaire stood at Muller's door 65, leering. The Floor 7's denizens peering over its round shoulders, ogling his room. Two men were lying on the cot. One with a porcelain dessert plate balanced on his bare chest. The other's vermillion lips were outlined with lightly browned meringue.

And the leather heels of the management clicked up the hallway.

Even *he* couldn't understand it.

GRIEF

"*I need a woman!*" he bawled.

She hadn't been dead but two days. One might have expected a whimper of grief, like "Christ, I miss her. What am I going to do alone?" I climbed out of bed and opened the door. He was standing naked in our hallway, his face pressed against the window glass; it buzzed.

"Go back to bed," I said. "Circumstance always looks better in the morning." I pulled the blind so the neighbors wouldn't see.

"You don't understand," he cried.

"It's what I'm discovering the older I become. I don't like surprises." I draped my arm about his shoulders and escorted him toward their bedroom . . . he bristled at its threshold.

"Her dresses. Her shoes. The toiletries on the bureau. Her undergarments in our chiffonier." He pulled away from me, and again wailed, "*I need a woman!*"

If he weren't my father, I would have laughed. Hell, every man I've ever known has felt that way at least once in his life. Why should my old man be any different? One humiliates himself among other men to ever admit this. So we murmur it to ourselves, more often than we like to admit perhaps.

There have been times lying alongside my wife of twenty years when I've smothered the identical cry . . . the need so profound that even a faithful spouse couldn't satisfy it.

"Look," I said, "there are plenty of single women out there, widows who would love to share your company. Women outlive men. You know that. They get lonely, too. So look on the bright side. You may have a whole new life ahead of you."

He wasn't buying it. "You don't understand."

"What don't I understand?"

"It's not about getting laid, James." The look he shot me was a rebuke.

"I didn't say it was."

"Your mother's just passed. Christ, give me some credit. You may not believe it, but I do have some self-respect, you know."

"I was talking about companionship."

"Yeah, yeah, I know. That's what they all say. Will you go in there and grab my briefs for me, please?"

As if his room had suddenly become radioactive. Moments later we were sitting opposite each other at the kitchen table. I'd put up some coffee. The irony of the scene was delicious. How many nights when I was a kid I'd wait up for him so I could tell him my girl problems. Christ, I was always torn up inside, and he had this calming influence . . . plus an uncanny way with women. They were beguiled, charmed by him. I knew that he saw several on the side. Mother always suspected it, but never chose to explore it. Obviously she didn't want the evidence.

"Hey, Pap, tell me what I should do?"

He'd reel off divers wise saws that more or less amounted to: "Be stronger than the opposite sex. Make like you can take 'em or leave 'em. Always have at least one other on the side. Don't make a big show of it—she'll scent the competition. Never, *ever*, let her think you'd die for her. Oh, you can bull-shit and say that you will, and all that *coo-coo*. But don't let your heart shit you—for it always will. This girl stuff . . . all very rudimentary, Son."

And the next morning I'd awake reborn.

Now, at the fall interval of his life, *his* dam had ruptured— brought on by Mother's death. Here's my father unable to sleep because he's blubbering "I need a woman!" and I'm trying to sober him up with Irish coffee. It's existential. What the hell was I going to tell him?

"Do you understand what I'm talking about, Son?"

"What about Mrs. Rapucci, Dad?"

"Fuck Mrs. Rapucci!"

We both laughed. That was a good sign.

"Well . . ." I said.

"You just don't get it. Come here." He took my hand and pulled me back up the stairs. We stood outside their bedroom again. "Go in there and pull open the top drawer of the chiffonier."

The room was dark save for the streetlight laying an amber puddle across the bed. One side slept in.

"Go on, open it."

Inside, neatly piled were panties, camisoles and slips, and—bunched in one corner—a cluster of brassieres. The drawer let loose a breath of sachet.

"That's what I'm talking about," he said. "Now, open the closet door. Go on, do it, James."

Plaid knife-pleated skirts, georgette shifts, crêpe de Chine empire dresses, blazers, all draped on wire hangers; mules, espadrilles, and spaghetti-strap heels assembled underneath. On the upper shelf—black-pill box hats whose veils she'd let fall at weddings or funerals. On his side, prosaic two-piece suits in summer and winter blends. The closet was redolent of gardenia.

"Do you get it yet, boy?"

He ambled back down the stairs.

"No damn way are we ever going to get rid of her presence. You can throw all that shit outside, clean every nook and cranny of her belongings, toss out the creams and face lotions, the prescription bottles, her Bible, her photograph . . . you name it. Scour her out of every board and the plaster in this house . . . and she still won't leave."

I poured us another coffee.

"*I need a woman*," he whispered, his face a hairsbreadth from mine.

"I don't get it, Pap. What are you telling me?"

"You really want to know?"

"This isn't like you."

"Do you grasp why she wore those things up there? That smoky sun dress with jasmine flowers, for instance? She'd stand there admiring herself in the mirror, watching me button it up her backside. Those peekaboo nets she'd drop over her china blue eyes. Undergarments the shade of her blush?"

"Why?"

"*So I wouldn't have to wear them.*"

"Yeah, I get it," I said. The damn whiskey was blubbering.

"Listen to what I'm telling you. *It's your mother's stain . . .*"

"Finish your coffee so we can go back to bed."

"No. You don't get it!" he bellowed, bounding out of his chair. A gingham napkin from the buffet drawer he tied under his chin—a babushka. Like she might have, he pressed his face to mine, and, *sotto voce,* mewled again . . . "*I need a woman.*"

I followed him up the stairs.

We entered the darkened room and in a fury Father snatched her garments out of the closet, the chiffonier, the bureau drawer—heaping everything onto the bed they had shared for decades. With each item his frenzy accelerated. The last garment on the clothes pole, a navy blue button-down-the-front frock with a stiff sailor's collar, he held up to his torso. "How about this, Junior, with my patent leather *please-fuck-me* shoes? Are my seams straight?" He turned like I'd witnessed her do many times, bending a calf up toward his derriere while staring over a bare shoulder.

The streetlight's corrugated shade serrated the room's shadows. With one swipe he pitched the bureau's opaque perfume bottles and pearly emollient jars across the floor and under the bed, a chromium lipstick tube the lone survivor. He opened it and studied himself in the mirror, my face his double.

Was he going to paint both our lips?

"Pap, please, stop this absurdity."

"I've no bosom!" he cried. "My chest is a goddamned void. Look at me!" A salmon brassiere dangled from his neck. The circle he'd drawn around his mouth exaggerated our pathos.

"What's left for me, James? Will she ever come home?"

Father lay down upon her wrappings, burying himself.

Grief.

Causes people to do the strangest things. His was implacable. I still had him. Her departure hurt, but I could abide it. Yet a piece of him was half gone. It was as if the heart was now eating itself in some kind of bizarre, comic remorse.

I slept downstairs that evening.

At first light I softly opened his door. Their room had been restored. Father was sound asleep. His frozen magenta "O" faintly smudged.

THE HIRELING

"I have just the man."

The dispatcher acted upon the flimsiest of evidence when he advised callers.

A surgeon wanted assistance dressing his foundation beds. I arrived to several yards of hemlock shavings pyramiding his driveway. A bright green wheelbarrow cradling a silver shovel sat alongside. All day I fed him the mulch. He insisted I leave the shovel in the driveway.

"I can't risk your using it anywhere near me. My hands are my life." At day's end we shared a pitcher of pink lemonade, and he paid me in paper dollars fingered out of a mason jar.

The second house sat alongside a steep wooded hill. The paterfamilias said he was hurrying off to the airport, but, "This is what I want done."

In rainstorms water sluiced off the ridge, washing away patches of their newly sodded lawn. A trailer load of paving bricks had been stacked in his driveway. "Take the bricks and construct a gutter down the incline, directing the water away from our residence and dooryard. You look like an intelligent young man with brawn."

I was protected from the sun by dense foliage, and, whereas the surgeon hadn't trusted me to wield a shovel in his proximity, this employer was giving me carte blanche to construct a Roman waterway.

At noon his young wife watched me leaning against my car, eating a sack lunch. "Won't you come inside?" she said. "It's air conditioned in here, and I've made iced tea."

The pair owned a handsomely appointed Tudor. A Picasso hung in the foyer, a Braque over the kitchen table. I identified them. She pointed to several other copies on their living room walls.

"Man Ray, Corot, Ben Shawn, and, yes, Matisse's *Boy at the Piano*. A favorite of mine, too," I said.

She buttered herself an English muffin. "What are you doing here, Mr. Hart?"

"Building a wonderful sluiceway down your hillside," I said.

"My husband doesn't even know these painters."

I didn't reply.

"Did you have enough to drink?" she asked, standing.

"Yes," I said, taking the remains of my lunch back outside.

With pick and mallet I traced the path the furrow would take down the ravine. Two yellow birch saplings I had to uproot. The channel the water had cut was virtually a straight chute from the crest to the dooryard. My masonry waterway would snake in wide and graceful curves through the maple, oak, and birch, to its end in a rubble catchall far removed from the house.

Day two the wife placed a milk bottle of iced tea alongside my car at noontime. I waved from the hillside shadows.

I began laying the bricks in the runnel on day three. The hillside wound was no longer a serpentine humus scar cleaving the deep green moss and leaf cover. The brick waterway opened wide at the chine, gradually narrowing until it began to twist and turn luge-like away from the house, hundreds of feet below. I didn't stop for lunch that day, the results to the eye so satisfying: a dust-red aqueduct, firm and unbroken against the vicissitudes of nature. It was looking ancient.

At half light the owner stood in the dooryard watching me lay the last brick.

"Why didn't you make it fall straight?" he asked, bemused.

I glanced up at his wife who stood watching us with her hands on the porch railing.

"Pay the gentleman, Frank. Or Man Ray will stop by for lunch." She found this very humorous, and waved her arms as if to dismiss us both. "Christ, it's lovelier! A Magritte appendectomy in our hillside. Besides, the guy knows every damn work of art we have hanging on our walls. I told you when you called the State Unemployment Office we might get more than you bargained for."

The very next morning as I sat waiting in the day laborer pool, the dispatcher summoned me forward again. "Hart, you know we do random checkups? The most recent missus had some good things to say about you."

"Oh, yeah?"

"She said you made a beautiful landscape painting. I thought I'd sent you out to dig a trench. What the hell did you do?"

"These people presume you hire out mules."

"Well, here—this one came in this morning."

"Where and what is it?"

"In Shadyside. They want a full-time gardener."

"I don't think I'm qualified."

"I inform them we only vouch for a man's willingness to work. Look, they get a horticulturist at minimum wages. You both win."

It's brick newly pointed, the Hubbard residence was a fine copy of a Samuel McIntire Federal with six over six fenestrations and enameled forest-green panel shutters set on an acre of land at the end of a cul-de-sac. A wooded conservation area bordered its property line. Both the husband and wife greeted me when I stepped out of my car.

"How do you do, Mr. Hart? We phoned your most recent reference. Our plantings are all rather proper, but frankly, both Lydia and I agree, uninspired. We need a resourceful hand to stamp these grounds with his personality.

"Your hours will be from eight to five, and any day it rains for more than two hours without interruption, you may go home.

We've set up a spare room for your use upstairs in the carriage house that has its own sink and commode. It also boasts a table and chair where you may eat your lunch—take one hour, please—or plan new flower beds. How does it sound?"

"I've very little experience in gardening. I'm merely a day laborer."

"Ah, dispense with the humility."

"Well, I am willing to study."

"There are source books in the carriage house. There's a pair of clean coveralls hanging up in there, too, if you don't mind. You'll be furnished a new change at least twice a week."

We shook hands.

"Your pay envelope will be waiting for you Friday mornings on our back porch in the event you want to make an errand that noon. Lydia will start you out in the a.m."

It's very difficult keeping a sense of who you are when others insist that you conform to their notion of themselves. The tan coveralls were British-made, had brass buttons, and a conceit of cuffs. In the carriage house sat several pairs of green Wellingtons, most of which fit. Lydia suggested that I begin by sprucing up the flower beds, deadheading the roses, and freshening the mulch about the foundation plantings. In the rear of the carriage house were slat bins of cedar, pine, and hemlock mulch, renewed each spring by a local nursery.

"If the heat becomes unbearable, Mr. Hart, I'd suggest you retire to your carriage house atelier and read up. If you are occupying your mind in our behalf, like studying horticulture, we know you are working."

One aspect of my duties, of course, was to keep their expansive lawns groomed. Except for the trim work where I used a finely tooled, again British made, push reel mower, I sat on a tractor that pulled several of them. Lydia described for me the lawn pattern that she and Elijah Hubbard wanted the mowers to lay down. The sketch hung in the carriage house, describing the quadrant where I was to begin, when to make turns, and where to close. The chiaroscuro looked like a grass quilt.

"You can tinker with the tractor, too, Mr. Hart. Make it hum to your satisfaction. That, too, is part of your job. If it takes a day getting it to work exactly to your satisfaction, so be it."

The second week of my employment, Lydia Hubbard had pinned a note to my change of coveralls.

"I'm having a few guests over for tea this morning, Mr. Hart. Around noon we will be traveling to Wayside Inn for lunch. I want you to chauffeur us. You needn't eat your lunch before as I've reserved a place for you there, too. Your outfit and cap you'll find in the closet in your room. The key to our Packard alongside. The purple coneflowers need weeding out. Perhaps you can cut the beds back and leave some transplants for my guests. I'd very much appreciate that."

I spent the morning spading the echinacea, tossing most of what I dug up in the compost bin. I did pot and set aside several clumps as she requested. A full-length mirror hung on the back of the closet door. Inside, a pair of black chauffeur breeches, one starched white shirt with black four-in-hand quick-tie, a double-breasted chauffeur's jacket, and a patent-leather billed cap. Leather leggings hung on a lone hanger.

At noon I pulled up to the house's porte-cochere. Mrs. Hubbard and her two lady friends I assisted into the back seat. A glass partition in the Packard separated the driver's compartment. I could barely hear the women's light banter over the hum of the twelve cylinder engine. Looking straight ahead, as I presumed a chauffeur would do, I drove with two hands on the wheel and arrived within the half-hour.

"Mr. Hart, when you are finished parking the automobile, go inside and tell the receptionist you're my chauffeur. She'll have a place waiting for you."

"Oh, please, ma'am. I'm not hungry."

"If we eat, so do you, sir. Come, ladies."

Louie the Fifteenth apple-green armchairs surrounding linen-dressed tables set with bone china, sterling silver, and crystal goblets, dotted the Wayside's cool interior. Its ceilings were uncustomarily low for an eating establishment of this caliber, but most of the patrons like Lydia Hubbard were over fifty. Women in stiff white shirts with bow ties and flared black skirts, waited on them. A Creole sang and played a medley from "Oklahoma" on a Bösendorfer at the far end of the room.

"Lydia Hubbard's man? Right this way please."

I was ushered into the kitchen. Identical table appointments, except the lone chair was a plain arrow back. The busboy attending Mrs. Hubbard's party served me, keeping me apprized of what courses the ladies were working on, and alerting me at the demitasse and dessert phase to warm up the car.

"They might treat themselves to a cordial today," he winked.

He returned with a shot glass of Grand Marnier. Alongside he placed two breath mints.

On the journey home, Mrs. Hubbard had me stop at a farm stand. After I deposited her guests at their estates, she slid open the glass partition and dropped a sack of unshucked corn alongside me in the passenger's seat. "Take the rest of the afternoon off, Mr. Hart. It was delightful; we must do it again soon."

So it is with some sadness and regret that I relate the following.

By the close of the initial month's employment, I'd amassed a considerable amount of know-how regarding horticulture. The first visible sign that the Hubbard's took delight in was when I moved the blue hydrangeas away from the yellow achillea. "I never did like that corner of the garden," Lydia exclaimed one morning. "It was a most gauche color combination."

That very same morning, I looked up from the foxglove bed and noticed a young man standing several feet away on the lawn eyeing me. He was about my age, and we shared the same build, hair color, and blue eyes.

"Hello. Who are you?"

"Toby," he said.

"Oh, a friend of the Hubbard's?"

"I've been watching you for several days." He spoke with the lilt of a young college professor. A certain irony in his voice, a playfulness in his mien.

"From afar?"

"Up there." He pointed to the rear of the McIntire house, the windows of the room on the second floor on its north-end corner. They were covered by green opaque window blinds.

"Learning my secrets, are you?"

"Yes." He shared the amusement.

"Did you catch me in the chauffeur's duds?"

"Charming. Mother drew my attention to you."

"Toby Hubbard?"

"Terence Edward Hubbard. And yours?"

"Buddy Hart."

"You been a gardener long, Buddy?"

"A month now. And you?"

He backed away, retreating into the shadows of the three massive willow trees that boarded the small stream running at the edge of their property.

I continued my work, planning to join him at lunchtime. But he wasn't about. At quitting time I glanced up at his room. One of the blinds had lifted, and he stood stiffly in it, wearing a pinstriped antique New York Yankee baseball uniform. As if he were a poster I was looking at pasted onto the glass.

Two days later, midmorning at the rose bed, Toby startled me once again.

"You're a professor, aren't you, Mr. Hart? Once fall begins, Mother will have you sit across the Chippendale dining room table from me and commence our tutoring sessions. I'm very much looking forward to it. I presume we'll begin with Qume and logic—our first course. Kant and Hegel, our second. Then begin to study Joyce and the *Odyssey*. About noon would be right when the sunlight is sparkling on the mahogany breakfront. Then we must break for a game of . . ."

"I'm the gardener, Toby."

"Just as easy being the professor, Mr. Hart. You'll find texts, a table, and a chair up inside the McIntire house, and a very pleasant reading lamp with a paper shade that casts a warm light over any text. In addition, there is a single bed covered with a log cabin quilt, and a cloth rug to protect your bare feet from the cold oak plank floors on damp mornings. Down the hall is a bathroom we will share. It has a key on the inside. We need never to intrude on the other.

"Do you have friends? Perhaps after our daily lessons, you could invite them over when Mother goes to her afternoon luncheons. We could gather in Father's den, sit in the overstuffed leather chairs, put our feet up on boar ottomans, smoke Cuban cigars, and listen to music of our own liking. I prefer Satie. How about you, Mr. Hart?"

From the back porch Mrs. Hubbard was watching Toby and me. Momentarily she stood next to him. "Come, Terence. There's no cloud cover today. I don't want you getting too much sun."

"What did he say to you, Mr. Hart?" She'd returned to the cream and strawberry lily bed upon leading Toby back inside the house.

"He wanted to know the botanical names of all the flowers, ma'am. I was teaching him what I'd learned."

"Oh," she said, nonplused. "By the way, Mr. Hubbard and I have been meaning to inform you that your hoary alyssum patch on the south side of the house is beginning to look scraggly. Will you attend to it, please?"

I'd heard it from other employers before. It was their tone. The householder with the copies of Braque and Man-Ray on her wall—she began counting the hours after our truncated lunch that noon. And Friday, when I'd customarily get to wear the chauffeur's costume, Elijah Hubbard came home early from work to accompany Lydia and the women to the Wayland Inn.

The following Monday, I noticed my coveralls were the soiled ones I'd taken off at week's end. I mowed the west lawn that morning, then proceeded to prune the rhododendron about the Federalist mansion.

"We must wear the same suit size, don't you think?"

His stealth unsettled me once again.

"Thirty-nine long?" I said.

"There's a tailored khaki gabardine two-piece along with a chamois-yellow shirt and rep tie inside a garment bag on the back seat of your automobile, Mr. Hart. I want you to have it."

"A rep tie, too, Toby?" I said, hoping to humor him.

"Princeton. It's where you went, isn't it? What was your eating club? Don't forget to invite the others, Mr. Hart. We'll sit in Father's study just like you said. I'll break out the gin and bourbon. Just men, now mind you. And brush up on your Hume and Locke. When the weather begins to turn, those texts look quite lovely lying about the empty rooms."

Lydia Hubbard was upon us.

"Mr. Hart, fall is imminent. There's a small bonus inside for you." She palmed me a tallow-yellow pay envelope. Toby had rushed back into the house. She in his draft.

I recovered my personal belongings from the upper room in the carriage house, and planned on hanging Toby's gift in its closet. But the back seat of my car was empty.

On the way out of the circular driveway, I glanced up at his north corner windows. He stood in the chauffeur's suit wearing a cracked smile.

QUEEN ESTHER

Perhaps the most interesting bureau drawer in Ben's mother's room was her unmentionables drawer. Most of the items looked fragile, the same shade of pink, coral and dusty rose, stacked in three rows like silk scarves. Further, once the compartment was drawn open, a sweet aroma wafted out of a calico sachet bag.

Petticoats, half slips, camisoles, panties, and, at the very bottom, the ballast—a chunky girdle festooned with bone stays, wire fasteners and elastic straps with catches that kept her nylon sheers from drooping like loose skin on her legs. "It doesn't belong here," thought Ben. He recalled an aged catfish he'd once pulled out of a pond with wire leaders and hooks decorating its mouth.

Ben had looked forward to this day. She'd promised the two of them were going on a special trip. He sat all dressed on the side of the fully made bed. His father had left early to hurry onto the golf course.

"Where are we going, Ma?"

"To a Queen Esther social."

Queen Esther was the name of her Sunday Bible class. All women, most of whom Ben thought looked like boarded-up Victorian houses. His mother was the youngest and prettiest in the group. He watched her draw cocoa stockings up her legs, careful so as not to cause them to run, then roll their ends in cloth covered rubber bands high on her thighs.

"Are the seams straight, Ben?" she asked. Lifting up the half slip.

"Yes," he said. She never asked his father.

"Ben, go get the clear nail polish."

He watched her dab its applicator brush on the snag that threatened to travel a cloud stream down her leg.

"What's a social, Ma?"

"An occasion when women get together."

"What do they do?"

"Oh, talk. Drink tea, and there will be much to eat." He'd seen the fresh macaroni salad sitting in a container in the refrigerator that morning.

"What will I do?"

It didn't matter, actually. When he was invited by his father to go someplace, it meant sitting on a barstool downing several fountain Coca-Colas while studying reflections of the patrons in the giant bar mirror. It was always dusky in those places, and smelled of Lysol. His father never wanted to leave. But he and his mother took long drives in the country; she'd turn on the car radio and sing like Jo Stafford. Sometimes she'd drive thirty miles to Warren, Ohio, to visit her aunt. Ben would walk down the street to the crossing and watch the freight trains move through. Alongside the tracks a black man owned a shack roofed with metal Royal Crown Cola signs; he sold bread, milk, candy, and soda chilled in an ice trough. Ben liked to go inside and "fish" for a bottle of lime green soda. The store had a dirt floor. Black children would fish with him in the soda trough, too. They liked purple soda.

"You will do what you've always done, Ben . . . stick by me."

The social was being held in a rambling Queen Anne Victorian with a grand wrap-around porch in a rural community called Harmony. Several wicker-back rocking chairs with peony cushions lined either side of the oval windowed entrance like hotel guests taking the morning sun. When the pair climbed the steps to twist the bell, Ben spotted goats in a penned enclosure alongside the driveway.

"See," she said, "I told you there would be something for you to do."

Ben immediately recognized Grace McKibben when the door opened, the president of the Queen Esther class. Except he was used to seeing her dressed in black wool, layers of it—blouse, cardigan sweater, a jacket, and skirt that fell just above a short expanse of her black cotton stockings and string-tied heels. A cameo brooch was the only color in the whole expanse of garments, and it rested tight against her Adam's apple. Mrs. McKibben always wore a pill box hat in church, too, with black netting over her chignon—a dark scrim that she might pull down over her chalky face at a moment's notice, he thought.

But this Saturday morning, she met mother and son at the door in a dress patterned with a riot of melon peonies, like those on the porch rockers' cushions, against an ivory background, and matching salmon satin slippers and hose. Stuck in her gray bun was a sprig of baby's breath.

"Welcome to Queen Esther's soirée!" exuded Mrs. McKibben.

"Oh, Grace, you look so beautiful," Ben's mother declared.

"What's a soirée?" he whispered as they were being escorted into the dimly lit vestibule.

"Shhhh," she admonished. "It's a woman's social. Now be on your best behavior."

It was a grand interior. A Matisse odalisque hung in the paneled hallway. Oriental carpets jeweled its dark parquet floors, and like young girls, huge Chinese jardinieres stood sentry at the living room entranceway. Ben could see perhaps a dozen women standing, talking to each other animatedly, all attired in muted spring dresses with white or pastel slippers. When the hostess opened the French doors, the fragrance of a sweet perfume momentarily overcame him.

"Katherine Daugherty and her Gainsborough son, Ben!" the hostess gushed. The women all turned and smiled at the pair, one of them commenting, "Oh, Katherine and Ben, we are so glad you came." Ben watched a fawn-colored Siamese cat with gas-blue eyes brush up against the shiny hose of several of the guests. Cookies and delicate pastries graced glass-topped tables throughout the grand room. At one end in a circular alcove with curved windows sat a home organ. Mrs. McKibben was the organist for the Second United Presbyterian Church.

"It looks like we're all here," the Bible class president declared. "Please sit down, ladies." Eyeing Ben standing at his mother's side— "and gentleman."

The room is as large as our downstairs, thought Ben. Tufted sofas, love seats and overstuffed chairs were backed up against oak wainscoting. Timbers lined the ceiling.

"We have some minor class business to conduct before we begin the SOIRÉE . . ." she hesitated, and several women giggled. Ben's mother smiled innocently, not knowing anything more than he did. "But before that, I want to introduce you to my dear friend and companion."

She opened the French doors to the dining room. A diminutive woman entered, perhaps a decade younger than the hostess, with marcelled raven hair, pale skin, and wearing a watery persimmon red lipstick. Mrs. McKibben wore no make-up, except white face powder.

"Lydia Hopkins, ladies." Miss Hopkins curtseyed. The Queen Esther president grasped her hand and directed, "Go bring in the tea, dear."

The woman was as young as his mother and, Ben thought, as attractive, too. "Where's Mr. McKibben, Ma?"

Katherine Daugherty scowled.

"Who takes care of the goats?" he asked.

"Ben!" she hissed.

Miss Hopkins wore a crisp white waitress' apron over a black shirtwaist dress. Its collar, unlike Grace McKibben's, was open and exposed a flushed expanse of flesh. She had a self-effacing manner, and was given to uttering short sentences.

"Oh, you're welcome. I'm sure."

"Yes, isn't it a lovely home? Grace has such exquisite taste."

"Oh, no, I didn't bake these brownies. Grace did. She's a marvelous chef."

"Does she take care of the goats?" Ben asked.

Lydia Hopkins, who stooped over to pour tea in their bone china cups, smiled. Katherine Daugherty grinned sheepishly.

"Oh, why are you so nosey?" She glanced up at Lydia, appealing for her understanding.

"Yes, I tend to the goats, Ben. I'll take you out to meet them later this morning."

He liked her right off. As the Queen Esther women palavered about the upcoming business of the Bible class, she'd periodically glance over at him and wink.

Soon the noise in the large room subsided. The hostess had excused herself minutes earlier, and her guests were all comfortably ensconced, waiting for the next turn of events. Ben fidgeted like it was getting stuffy.

There were occasional puddles of hushed conversation, but most of the women sat decorously mum, a few studying the sunlight filtering through the stained glass window over the double keyboard organ. When, stunningly, Grace McKibben swaned through the dining room doorway bedecked in a bottle-green velvet chapeau festooned with plastic cherries, one banana, and an orange. Throwing her arms wide, she kicked off her salmon slippers and cried:

"Welcome to Queen Esther's Soireé!"

The ladies burst into laughter that sounded more like delighted squeals.

President McKibben sat down at the organ, and broke into a rousing chorus of "Mississippi Mud."

As she furiously pedaled, and pushed and pulled at the concert stops—the living room literally swelling with brass instrumentation—an undernourished Aunt Jemima shimmied into the gathering wearing a red bandana—just like on the box of pancakes Ben loved so. Lydia Hopkins' milky white face, now marred with burnt cork, and in her hands—bones.

At the nodding of Mrs. McKibben, Lydia obliged her accompanist with a stiff one minute jig and rib-clapper percussion.

The women were in titters.

Lydia curtseyed once again. When the ringmaster held her hands high in the air, requesting silence, Ben wondered if they'd visit the goats with Lydia wearing blackface.

"Ladies," Mrs. McKibben barked, "Now for the surprise. Queen Esther's Morality Play! But you must all take part." Conspiratorially, she swept her chignon about and glared at each woman assembled. "But never breathe a word of this to any of our congregation. We've survived for thirteen years through ecclesiastical famine and scarce liturgical fortune. But the God of Mercy loves each and every one of us. Pray and be merciful, He admonishes. *And, above all, HAVE INNOCENT FUN!*"

The ladies applauded, even Ben's mother. The cat jumped up between the pair and rolled its back into his side. Ben thought the shade in the room had become rosier. As if the sky outside had begun to bleed salmon. The floral upholstered furniture . . . all of it gave off a pale carnation glow just as did the soft-hued women's dresses. The tinted flesh of the photographs hanging on the wall. The painting over the fireplace—a pink calliope unicorn. The coral bordered carpet in the grand living room with a mimosa center. Peach roses now began opening in their crystal vases, releasing their perfume. Ben, wishing he were outside with the goats, and slowly succumbing to the chamber's rising temperature.

Lydia Hopkins opened the double glass doors to the hallway, and switched on the tear-drop chandelier, illuminating a wide staircase with fanciful mahogany balusters. It was as if the women were sitting below a proscenium arch.

The audience was aroused by the sound of bells Ben had heard on horses pulling wagons for hay rides. Leather belts festooned with silver balls inside which rolled steel bearings. The straps shook several times, to announce an appearance. All eyes were fixed on the upper level of the staircase illuminated by a stained glass window.

Lydia Hopkins cried out: "QUEEN ESTHER!"

About her neck a black strap of Christmas bells, and scantily attired in a champagne brassiere, one of those catfish-hooked girdles with catches to which her black mercerized hose were fastened, and no shoes . . . her pasty flesh, mounds of it, harnessed by the unmentionables, brocaded and laced but still looking very much like saddles or straps . . . Grace McKibben held aloft two tambourines like the tablets of Moses. Each step she descended, the harness bells jangled, accompanied by a furtive glances she, Queen Esther, shot to her admiring, but noticeably embarrassed, dark-faced Lydia.

The Bible class, at first stunned, gradually effected a smattering of nervous laughter. When Grace reached the last step, they were applauding. Ben heard the goats bleating in the dooryard. Without any prodding, the auburn-haired women sitting alongside Katherine Daugherty darted into the dining room towards the back stairway. Momentarily, she, too, appeared on the upper landing, slapping her hand against a pressure cooker she'd lifted on her way though the kitchen. She wore no shoes or stockings, a purple petticoat, and had a carrot stuck in her hair.

The guests egged her on as she flounced down the steps. Soon the women were waiting in line to be the next on the illuminated stairway. The hilarity was building.

Grace McKibben and Lydia sat on carpeted Kurdistan cushions in the vestibule, clapping robustly for each grand entrance.

Another member of the Bible class (Ben recognized her as the Union Trust bank teller's wife, Sylvia Lowell) poised on the landing behind an ironing board, her dancing partner. Out and in she moved it in clipped tango fashion, to the snapping of fingers in the audience. You couldn't see her entire body until she begin to do a liquid turn as she and the dancing board "male" descended the oaken stairway as partners. She wore Titian-shaded panties, and for Ben's sake, one presumed, spools of thread cellophane-taped to her nipples.

Ben had forgotten the goats. He couldn't even hear them. *Would his mother dare do it?* The women all around her were plotting, getting ready. Finally, one of the last, Katherine Daugherty rose. Ben stood up, too.

"I want to do it," he begged. She shook her head and sat him back down. The women snickered. Soon she, too, appeared at the top of the stairs in a red and white gingham tablecloth.

"Ohhhh," her classmates teased, as if they were men. Katherine Daugherty held up her hand to silence the impatient, and with cunning deliberativeness, pealed the tablecloth off her body. Instead of panties, she wore a flour sack dishtowel diaper and copper wire pot scrubbers she'd strung over her breasts with kitchen twine. From behind her back she proffered an iron, and at each stair pantomimed steaming the creases out of her thighs and derriere.

The assembled stood and huzzahed. Ben heard the goats bleating. *What if Mr. McKibben comes home?* he worried.

The last member of the Queen Esther class to descend the stairs was Pastor Rose's wife, Blanche, who'd tied a length of clothesline about her upper torso and another about her waistline. To cover her bodice she'd attached labels from canned goods to the rope by clothespins. Over one breast was a Del Monte Corn label, the other—Campbell's Pork and Beans. Two clothespins held the crushed tomato labels over her pelvis, front and rear.

The congregation had finally spent itself.

Gathered closer together—huddling actually—in the center of the capacious living room, they sat with their legs folded beneath them, some on pillows, still wearing their improvised costumes, or wrapped in bed sheets that Lydia had supplied. The detritus of domesticity—sundry pans, scrubbers, iron, ironing board, clothesline, clothespins, ersatz fruit—and even silk panties, girdle and one camisole—lay in a heap over by the organ.

They ate coleslaw, macaroni salad, potato salad, and baked beans on paper plates served by Miss Hopkins, who by now had cold cream buttering her face. Coffee was perking in the huge metal church urn in the kitchen. Katherine Daugherty made a plate of food for her son, who sat off with the cat, wondering if Mr. McKibben might take him out to tend the goats. It felt like it was getting that time of day. The dusty rose atmosphere in the room had begun to give away to a chromatic blue, and the strong fragrance of lavender sachet had evaporated . . . perhaps much earlier when Ben was watching the stairway show. Shadows had converged on the room. Several of the assembled looked pale under their sheets; others shivered in their unmentionables.

Katherine Daugherty finally stood, and gathered her clothes. The rest of the Queen Esther Bible Class did likewise.

"Oh, Ben, we didn't even get to feed the goats, did we," Lydia said. "You come again. We'll do it first thing."

Mrs. McKibben hovered behind her. "Did you enjoy Queen Esther's soirée, son?"

"I did," he said.

"Now you won't breathe a word of it, promise?"

He nodded.

"Scout's honor?"

Ben extended his index and middle finger.

"You're still a little man. That's why your mother let you attend. We don't permit grown men in Queen Esther's Bible class."

He could understand why.

THE AVENGERS

I've fantasized about sex, but not about murder.

Never owned a gun. Jimmy hadn't, either. The day I told him, he went out and bought a snub-nosed .38 revolver.

"What time do we meet in the city?"

"I'm ready to leave now," I said.

"I phoned work. Told them an emergency came up in the family. Hoped to be back in a week."

"I did the same. But we have to have a strategy. We just can't go into the woods and shoot."

"Don't worry, I'm cool."

I hadn't heard that tone of voice since the night years earlier he'd returned home from boot camp. After supper, at his challenge, we began wrestling in the dining room. Always I could pin him down. Within minutes he'd straddled me and was bending the fingers of my left hand back toward my elbow.

"Enough, I give up."

"Huh-uh. You got to say *Uncle*. Nice and sweet like."

"You're going to break them, you little prick!"

"Easy with the harsh words now." The fingers arced farther back. "*Uncle*. Say it, Buddy. Let me hear it."

"UNCLE!"

"Much better." His smile revealing a splinter of teeth. "*Semper Fi.*"

He ate his dessert. Red Jell-O with a slice of pineapple and a dollop of mayonnaise.

"You would have snapped the bones, huh?"

"You do what you must. No offense."

Would we have bought the gun and ammunition if it had been a less heinous rape?

In an adjoining Costa Del Sol hotel room late one evening, I heard an earnest voice, a matron on night duty perhaps, console a young woman who had been sexually assaulted moments earlier on the beach. The victim was sobbing and retching.

"You'll get over it, honey. We all do."

Many predators on the beach at night. Never advertised.

I wouldn't have called my brother. Except Helen was hurt.

"Do we work at night?"

"You know the city. Make the hotel arrangements. By the time we meet I'll have our plan of action. I know how sensitive you are about such matters—so I'll pull the fucking trigger, too." His icy flash of humor.

"There were seven of them."

"What can she recall?"

"The leader—head shaved with the physique of a football player. Wore army fatigue pants, white sneakers that were spotless. As the mayhem was unfolding, Helen focused on his shoes. Would blood drip on them?"

"Who else?"

"The guy who spotted her stepping out of a taxi. Fancy brown and white shoes, matching royal blue slacks and summer blazer, white shirt open at the collar. Pomade on his hair. Slippery."

"Go on."

"She and her mother are partying. It's after midnight. Helen wants more vodka. Takes a twenty out of her mother's purse and hails a cab. (They lived in the fifties, NYC.) At some point she checks the meter, and realizes if she keeps riding she won't have enough money for the booze. 'Let me out.' She's now in the South Bronx. The Good Samaritan approaches and asks her why she is alone 'In this place, at this hour?'

"'I need to be shown the subway entrance,' she says."

"I don't want to fucking hear."

"I didn't either."

"Go on."

"The young man takes her by the arm and begins escorting her down Third Avenue. That's when the jackal, followed by others, slides out between two buildings.

"'Who's the chick? You been holdin' out on us?'

"Before she could run into the street, the pack closes in and hustles her into an abandoned lot. The bald one shoves Helen to her knees. He wants 'head.' She bites him. Enraged, he rips off her skirt and underpants, throws her face-down to the ground, and begins to sodomize her. He's unable. A switchblade opens and he inserts it into her rectum. Now he can."

"What's the Good Samaritan look like?"

"A choir boy."

"Did he partake?"

"Number seven. At some point he returns alone and drags her out to the curb where a cabby finds her unconscious and hemorrhaging."

"You know where she first got off on Third?"

"The very spot."

"We don't have to get all seven. I'll aim for the ringleader."

"How will you know?"

"Trust me."

"Helen wasn't the first. The jackal pulled a tube of KY Jelly out of his fatigues."

I shivered when I repeated that.

"Wear your old clothes, Buddy. We got to look like we know the streets."

"Do you really want to go through with this?"

"Why'd you phone me?"

"What options do I have?"

"What'd Helen do to deserve this, Buddy?"

I'd no answers.

"First we blow his dick off. While he's squealing, I'll press the cold steel to his temple—and unload. Watch me, Buddy. You just fucking watch me."

Helen phoned me from the hospital the day after the incident.

"It's when I could no longer see the white shoes, and drowning in my own vomit, that I lost consciousness."

"What are the police doing?"

"A woman detective's been here most of the morning, pushing me for details."

"I don't know what to say."

"It's over now. I'm alive. I'll heal."

"I want to kill, Helen."

"So does she, Dad. She's on a mission."

So were we.

Sixteen years he and I shared the same bed. Countless nights dreaming about what we were going to do when we grew up. Talked endlessly about girls and automobiles. And when either one of us was hurt or slighted, the other would seek retribution.

Once, he attended a party on the North Hill—the wealthy section of Hebron. We always borrowed the old man's dress shoes for such occasions. He had to stuff newspaper in the toe boxes. A jock made fun of "Shorty's clown shit-kickers" in front of the girls. That night Jimmy beat the wall.

A year later I made love to the athlete's squeeze. While she was climbing back into her clothes, I said, "Tell Jake that Buddy Daugherty parked 'Shorty's shit-kickers' under your fucking bed tonight. OK?"

But it wasn't like wasting somebody.

Grown men, one a college professor, the other an administrator for a metropolitan hospital. Vigilantes. Plotting a stakeout in a third-floor room of the Chelsea Hotel in Manhattan. We'd dress in black. Jimmy carried the .38 for protection.

I visited Helen at Columbia Presbyterian each afternoon. We seldom discussed the incident. Now twenty-four and sharing an apartment with her mother upon graduating from college, she talked about wanting to kick the alcohol habit. The pair had become drinking buddies.

The first night of our reconnaissance, we parked outside the exact address on Third Avenue: a neon sign on the bar's windowless facade read "LELÉ da CUCA." Across the street, boarded-up storefronts, and at the end of the block—the lot overgrown with brush, ailanthus trees, and pocked with clothing, bottles, syringes.

Jimmy coiled his hand about the .38 in his pocket. We spotted vagrant types, but nobody matching the clear pictures in our minds. The Ivy Leaguer would have looked as out of place in the neighborhood as we did.

On day two and three we waited after dark for hours in a rented car two storefronts up from the bar. *Nothing.* While each noontime I sat with Helen, encouraging her to attend AA meetings and to leave her mother's apartment. "I'll help you. It's all going to get better."

My brother grew more steely. As boys we built guns that shot inner-tube bands, becoming fairly adept at refining their accuracy. We'd construct makeshift camps among the alders. Friends would divide into "armies," and set out to kill the enemy.

Day four, Jimmy looked like a killer.

"We got to make this happen. The fuckers are around here somewhere. We must smoke them out of their holes."

I was going the other way. That morning, Helen informed me the detective had a solid lead on the Ivy Leaguer. *"Helen, tell me all that you remember once again about the Samaritan,"* she queried.

"I told you everything I remember."

"Do you remember any jewelry he was wearing?"

"I can't."

"Did he ever use the word 'Ma'am'?"

"I don't understand."

"Like, 'Can I help you out, Ma'am?'"

"It's what he whispered, Dad . . . *'I'll go easy, Ma'am.'"*

The police suspected the son of a prominent employee of the city's court system. A year earlier he'd run afoul of the law in a South Bronx hit-and-run incident with a stolen vehicle.

"Tomorrow she's bringing photographs."

"Will you be able to identify any of them?"

"I'm better at remembering scents. The jackal reeked of Old Spice. The Good Samaritan, camomile. And the shadows—*sweat*."

In the car that night I told Jimmy. "A judge's son. Can you believe it?"

"Look who's stepping out of the bar, Buddy!"

The neon light illuminated the leader's bald pate . . . a perfect target. He was looking up and down Third Avenue, wearing the camouflage fatigues. I froze. I wanted to aim for the crotch, severing his cock. We'd shove it down the bastard's gullet until he choked to death. As I sat there fantasizing, Jimmy held the .38 to the passenger's door window.

"What are you doing?"

"Practicing."

The jackal moseyed back into the bar.

"Tomorrow, Buddy."

Whereas in previous nights we paced the hotel room and slept in our clothes, this evening we showered and groomed ourselves before crawling in.

"Tomorrow you tell Helen goodbye. No one will be the wiser. Remember, no emotion, Buddy. You want the sonofabitch to suffer. So do I. Can't let ourselves get caught up in that shit. To win. *Icy. You got to be icy*.

"When I pop him, KY slumps over dead—and we rubber out. We don't tell anybody. Except telling ourselves that we did the right thing. OK?"

I couldn't back out now. But I knew the deliverer would cave. His jurist mother had too much at stake. The authorities would send him to some easy-time upstate facility. He'd finger the beast, then it was up to the police to round up the pleasure riders.

My brother wouldn't have to kill.

The next morning Helen identified the Good Samaritan. At noon a warrant was issued for the arrest of the jackal and his associates for attempted murder.

"He did knife you, Helen. They left you for dead," the detective reassured.

Jimmy wasn't listening when I climbed into the car.

"Do they got him?"

"No, but they have a warrant out for him."

"So do we, Buddy. So do fucking we."

He drove the black Ford up Broadway. Not a word passed between us. It was the big test between brothers. Forget about avenging the rape of my daughter. This was another drama. *Was I chicken shit or wasn't I?*

Seldom did anybody get hurt when we were boys. Big relief valves, those boastings. *"I'll kill the cocksucker! Tell him his big brother's going to cut his dick off!"* Cheaper than nickel cakes. We all thumped on our bony chests.

And the Marines, yeah, Jimmy learned something lethal there, too. Come a time in a young man's life when he must take a stand . . . *laws or no laws.* "The one place we never retreat is when our women are in play."

Justice could do what it damn pleased.

"What if we get caught?"

"Buddy, if you don't want to go through with this—get the fuck out of the car now. *She's my niece.* If you haven't got the balls to do what every self-respecting father should do . . . then fuck off, I'll uphold the Daugherty honor. *What will it be?*"

"Drive."

At Morningside Heights he had to pull over for a passing siren. "I simply asked, James, if you're prepared to spend a decade—or more—in prison?"

"Each fucking day a proud one." He placed the .38 on my lap and pressed the accelerator.

LELÉ da COCA's neon light bled a pulsing heliotrope wash over the stucco facade.

"I'll stand in that doorway next to the bar. You keep the car running. He steps out looking for somebody. Who the fuck knows who? When I pick the time . . . and I think the coast is clear . . . the Quantico medals I'll earn. Keep the car door open. We'll never look back. You ready?"

Jimmy stepped out of the car and leaned inside the entranceway of the adjacent building. Curly hair and a Tony-Curtis resemblance belied his assassin's black garb. He smoked with his left hand while grasping the .38 in his right pants pocket.

In forty-five minutes he smoked at least five Lucky Strikes. Nobody had either entered or left the bar. At exactly eight forty-five, LELÉ da COCA's doorway swung open. The jackal stepped out onto the sidewalk, glancing in the direction of the vacant lot. The gaseous neon mirrored his head heliotrope.

I depressed the accelerator, wanting to confirm the motor's life. Jimmy stubbed out a cigarette, and signaled me—while steadying himself against the entryway. He withdrew the .38.

Across the street someone shouted, "JESUS!"

Jimmy hesitated.

"It's me. *Lawrence*."

"My man! What you got?"

"Come see."

Jimmy's hand welded to the piece. The car revved. Jesus, with a swagger and bleach-white shoes, approached the Samaritan.

"Who you sharing tonight, *Mr. Lawreeeence*!"

With Grocks drawn, four plainclothes officers encircled the pair. Within moments the beast sat handcuffed in the back seat of an unmarked cruiser that had been idling across Broadway.

Jimmy jumped back into ours. "*Whew!* Turn on the radio." He tossed the .38 onto the floor of the back seat. "Christ, I ain't been so wound up since I left Quantico. *That was smooth, wasn't it? That's how you got do it, Buddy!*

"Damn, we missed our calling. Wouldn't you say?"

TRACKS

He discovered them early spring. His father had passed away one week before Christmas. Sometime before then, and following the first heavy snowfall, John Perkins had taken a stroll out to the copse of poplars, then swung back toward the house. In April the footprints would be erased.

Elijah sat in the kitchen the morning of his discovery, waiting.

"They look fresh," he thought. Clearly the imprint of the Wellington sole was the deceased's. How often had he tramped behind his father in wintertime, stepping in his prints, sometimes up to his knees? Back into the poplar stand hunting rabbit tracks. A double-barreled Boss shotgun cradled in his father's left arm.

Soon he'd hear the boots stomped free of snow, an audible shiver, the mackinaw landing on the clothes pole. Then, "Elijah? Is coffee up?"

The perked aroma couldn't mask the stale odor of the dead man's rooms.

Elijah took the mackinaw off the hook. Sitting on the mud-room bench, he pulled on the Wellingtons and tucked his pant legs inside. In the wide expanse of field behind the Tudor, John Perkins' were the only markings. Elijah stepped with care so that every seating was precise. Thirty yards out he stopped. The right and left foot tracks were aligned together, like shoes parked at the foot of a bed.

"What do I do now?" he thought.

A blue jay flew overhead, the leafless canopy crackling in the March wind. "What was he looking at?"

In the snow glazing, a vertical slit—as if John Perkins had taken a stick, stabbed, then pulled it back toward him a foot. "A gash in a wedding cake," Elijah mused.

Off to his right, the Wellington dance chart: *left forward, right forward, glide sidewards, and stop.*

Beyond this, the tramp resumed back toward the house.

Elijah dropped knee-first into the snow to explore the slash. "Was he drawing a word? And why the erratic Quick Step?" Where it appeared his father had withdrawn the marking instrument, several perforations followed in one and two inch intervals.

Elijah glanced up through the limned poplars and began laughing.

"He heard no word. No sudden knife of wind making him pause. It was the damn Java!"

Unzipping his trousers, he studiously intersected his father's cut of months earlier. Only his trajectory of the snow cross bled yellow.

The tracks back to the house were closer together now, not the relaxed gait that led them both into the copse.

"Father's trot, all of scarce seconds—had he known that instead of rabbit tracks, I would find his?"

Stamping the snow off the Wellingtons, he threw the mackinaw on the hook, and called out through the empty rooms: *"Is the coffee up? Elijah?"*

• • •

When Elijah related the story to me, I, like he, was haunted by the image: father interred, only to discover, months later, tracks outside the kitchen door heading off into the woods.

I've followed my brother's and my father's wake.

It's not unusual for me to hear one of them calling at night. *"Just over the ridge. Over here. What the hell's the matter with you? Are you blind? Here, goddamn it, over here!"* I move in the direction of

the voice, but when I think I'm there—nothing. A meadow of alfalfa and goldenrod, or a clothes closet stuffed with suits and shoes.

A meadow, because that's where my kid brother immolated
himself. Well, off to its side, before he ran through the hay aflame,
trailing a scar down its center. His car had run out of gas, and he'd
borrowed some from a nearby farmer. While priming the carburetor, he spilled it on his pant legs; before he stepped on the starter,
he lit a cigarette. That's when the ball of flames blew him out of the
front seat. God knows where he began running—perhaps to where
he thought he heard Father's voice.

I haven't seen either of them up-close yet. Suspect I will soon. John
Perkins summoned his blue-eyed Elijah into the copse of poplars.
Except our old man never carried a shotgun. Could have cared less
about rabbit or deer tracks. Spiked heel markings, yes. He'd follow
those anywhere, hearing their clicking on a sidewalk, or up a set of
stairs. I trail the scent of women into some dusky bar or a roadside
tavern. Huddled in the corner booth with one hand on a drink, the
other on a knee or thigh, he greets:

"*This way, Son. Just over the ridge.*"

Brother James echoes, "*Pap, Westley can't see.*" As if death was
a fiery stranger, he took it into his arms and kissed its mouth until
his red hair caught orange.

"*What's wrong, Westley, you afraid what's over the ridge? It's just
the old man and me.*"

Father never rebukes James' taunts. "*This way, Son, over the
ridge.*"

Darkness all about me, I pull myself forward, grabbing onto
exposed roots, their soil eroded by torrents of spring. As I get closer,
his voice becomes more distinct. "*That's it. Keep climbing.*"

I hear James laughing. "*He won't do it, Pap,*" he rags. "*He hasn't
got the balls that you or I did. Watch you don't slip, Westley.*"

But at the sky stands Father's clothes closet. Suit jackets I'd slip
on as a boy, imagining how many lifetimes it would take before
my hands grew out of their sleeves. And in its drawers—one with
a checkbook and stack of bills he'd been meaning to pay; below,

monogrammed handkerchiefs; then the sock and underwear drawer; finally, one containing a metal box, always locked. The suits fit
fine, except they're decades old. Creditors long since deceased. And
inside the cache box—an Elgin watch, its alligator strap seared,
handed to Father the day of James' immolation.

On his closet floor, a pair of golfing shoes, caked with mud. I
bring one to my nose. A scent of smoldering earth lingers at its
cleats. Wandering off the golf course that afternoon, he tramped
the lesion my brother left in McClusky's hay.

Like changes of skin, the garments hang in an orderly row—the
dark wool giving way to light poplin. All facing west. Squeezing
them in my arms, I ask, "Where are you? Your tracks stop here."

"Over the ridge," he answers.

• • •

This morning I look down at my hands, and see telltale signs of *his*
taking form.

As I work my way through each day, I no longer must stand
alongside women to recall the sorghum of life, sweetness of cou-
pling—the dying of a thousand times in one's arms . . . on this side
of the ridge, I savor the bouquet. Each is none the wiser of my theft.

Oh, he is growing inside me. I've become the fecund loam in
which he's rooted. The eyes, soon they, too, will skim over like sour
milk. But he always saw clearly. When he couldn't—he felt and
breathed.

James—my salamander? That slash he burnt in the meadow?
Nothing's grown there since fire dripped off his legs and hands
like blood. Seeding the grasses, alfalfa, and goldenrod, with his in-
trepid will to fornicate the earth back alive. To dance with the sun
until it dimmed, to ride the spikes of the stars until they broke into
spears of ice. We'll meet up in due time. He'll have man-stories
to tell, heading out long before I considered it was time to put my
mind to it.

But first the metamorphoses must occur.

When I see tracks in the snow one of these winters, when I plant my feet carefully inside each as I walk toward the copse in our woods up the rise, when I see where they hesitate, and a line— perhaps the first stroke of a word—is scratched in the snow, and when I see the simple two-step illustrated alongside . . . I'll know I'm close.

It is then I'll remove my shirt and pants, place my shoes under the nearest poplar, and write with orange ichor the color of my brother's *yes,* before vanishing over the ridge.

THE ROOMING HOUSE

Mrs. Vautier, the landlady, lived alone on the first floor of her two-story Queen Anne Victorian. She had four rooms to let on the second floor, serviced by a single bathroom, tub but no shower. One reached the attic rental up a narrow circular stairway.

I occupied the smallest room on the second (its curved sash window looked out upon railroad tracks) that barely accommodated a studio bed, an overstuffed dun-colored mohair chair and a metal clothes closet. The room's singular source of heat was a cast iron hot plate with starfish burners. In wintertime I stored perishables in a milk crate on the porch roof outside the large window.

In the tenancy alongside mine, on Sunday mornings, a woman and her lover would rendezvous. The walls were thin, so I'd take a stroll in the park. Across the hall lived a boarder who stood six and a half feet tall and taught machine shop at a local high school. A garrulous man, Ostrovsky was forever knocking on my door. Often in the evening he'd prepare dinner for two and leave my portion wrapped in tinfoil on a tray in the hallway.

In the room alongside him, I believed Mrs. Vautier stored her valuable antique furniture.

A female tenant that Ostrovsky and I'd never laid eyes on lived in the garret. We were convinced she'd linger at the attic landing, waiting until we had shut our doors, then scuttle down to use the bathroom. Mrs. Vautier had a penchant for using pastel colored toilet paper. The mystery attic boarder wrapped bobby pins in twists of toilet tissue—pale lime, or anemic strawberry—and slipped them under my door after dark.

Overhead, two recordings played continuously throughout the night: Mozart's *Klaiversonata* and Eric Satie's *Gynopodies*.

At various intervals of my aloneness, I fantasized that she was an exceedingly lovely Pre-Raphaelite and that her music was meant to entice me to ascend the garret stairs. As if incensed candles and a carafe of rosé wine would be waiting alongside her bed. In my most fevered imagination I could see myself boldly climbing the stairs. In fact, I never dropped a foot on the first one. When I inquired elliptically of Mrs. Vautier the identity of the attic boarder, she responded with equal disguise:

"I'm not a matchmaker, Mr. Daugherty. What my tenants do on their own behalf is their business. Collecting your rent is mine."

Ostrovsky wasn't interested in women. Mysterious ones or not. I'd hear male voices in his room, particularly after midnight on weekends. At daybreak one Saturday morning, vacating the bathroom, I saw his door open and a hardy young man in his early twenties appear. Ostrovsky was sitting on the edge of his bed with a pastel towel about his hairy waist. The visitor rushed down the outside steps.

"Oh, Daugherty, I should have introduced the two of you. That was my son, Leo. Doesn't look anything like his darling father, don't you agree?"

Not wishing to waste the morning palavering, I waved.

"How 'bout if I make us both breakfast? I've fresh sausages on the roof."

The stench of gelled grease from his infrequently washed pans and utensils made me nauseous. (We washed our dishes in the bathtub.)

"I want to finish another chapter this morning, Ostrovsky."

"Oh, that goddamn book of yours," he minced. "Worse than being henpecked by some old bitchy wife. Nothing good will come of it, Daugherty. You got to learn how to live."

I'd pull my door shut, then softly turn the latch. I was reluctant to hurt him. Actually he was one of the few friends I had. On the nights he entertained, I went out looking for female companionship in the local cocktail lounges. I was ashamed to bring a guest back to the boarding house. He had no such scruples.

But then again, I hadn't just been liberated from a two-decade old marriage that had deteriorated into acrimony and ice. Frankly, I enjoyed living alone for a change, and relished closing the door to my room, not having to answer to anybody except my solitary self. I could sit and write long into the darkness if I so chose, without Ruth banging on my door, yelling for me to stop.

I didn't even long for Ruth's body as I once had. Now it looked like a feathered-lure. Something I'd have to pay dearly for if I partook. Bait with a razor hook secreted inside that I'd be unable to rip out of my psyche. No, it wasn't difficult in our final months to lie opposite her on our bed, then turn away as she dressed for work. *Yes, dress it up,* I thought, *make it more alluring. Somebody will pay.*

So much better to endure the scent of rancid pork chop grease, the gas blue and yellow flames leaping out of the starfish burners warming my room. And me alone to dream about asphyxiation, stories and characters and rooms which the mind could enter or depart at will.

God knows I didn't miss her. But I did our two children. Sundays, when the neighboring boarder opened her body to her secret lover—and I'd vacate my room to stroll through the local park— I'd stop several houses down from my old apartment. Loitering in the shadows on the opposite side of the street, I hoped my daughters would be out in the yard playing. I didn't want them to spot me.

Why? Where could I take them? Back to Mrs. Vautier's? Better they get used to living with their mother. One day I'd make it right and return for them. What's more, I had to finish my book.

The smaller, Lucy, standing in the prior year's Easter raspberry jacket with the bone buttons and fur collar, her nose running, watching her sister. Grace, too, was dressed in her Sunday school indigo velvet dress, dirt about her mouth and nose, furiously digging for something. The squirrel's nuts?

Was I unhappy, or were they? Bleak as Sunday mornings often are, and especially gray. Where was their mother? An unfamiliar car sat parked outside her three-story apartment house. Was she still in bed like the lover whose *yes* I was attempting to escape this morning? Grace, now on her knobby knees, her white anklets slipping down into her black patent and leather shoes. (Always, I was stopping on our walks, yanking the stockings back up, and within a dozen steps they'd disappear again revealing her bare ankles.) Now, like some animal, her two fists about an oak branch, scraping the dirt daemonically. Lucy, unfazed, staring blankly into the empty street. Mucus rivulating evenly down her lips.

That morning I didn't go to the park but turned back to Mrs. Vautier's. Ostrovsky heard me coming up the outside stairs and met me on the landing.

"Oh, Jesus, I'm glad you're back."

"What is it?" I said.

He took me by the hand, normally a gesture I would have resisted. "We got a problem."

"We?"

"Uh-huh. Go over there by the door next to mine and take a deep breath."

"Over by the storeroom?"

"Isn't no storeroom, Daugherty. Go on, do what I tell you."

The odor was quite distinct. One that I'd never experienced. Unpleasant, considerably worse than any odor that had ever emanated from Ostrovsky's domicile.

"What is it?"

"Mr. Dobbs."

"Who?"

"All dressed up for his Sunday walk." Ostrovsky, with a flourish, opened the fourth room's door. There, lying on a puce chenille bedspread in the morning sunlight, lay a corpse, fully dressed in a navy blue pinstripe suit with a white linen pocket square, bow tie and black oxford captoes. A gray fedora sat before the chest of drawer's oval mirror.

"Christ almighty, Ostrovsky!"

"Poor bastard. I'd say he's been lyin' there for a week."

"I thought the room was stuffed with old furniture. I'd never seen anybody go in or out."

"Daugherty," he gestured to the attic, "lots of strange people in boardinghouses like this one. Kept his room neater than a pin, though."

"Does Mrs. Vautier know?"

He shook his head. "I wouldn't have either if the stench finally didn't get to me. I'm surprised it didn't get to you, Daugherty."

"Who's going to break the news?"

"We both will," he said, leading me down the inside steps to her quarters. He knocked on the door.

Mrs. Vautier was cool, as if this had happened before. Her first response, after gravely shaking her head: "Help me get him on the porch. I don't want him stinking up that room any more than he already has."

The three of us hurried back up the stairs, and with Ostrovsky at Mr. Dobbs' head, me at his feet, and Mrs. Vautier opening the door, we trundled him down the outside stairway, depositing Dobbs on her metal porch glider. She covered his body with the chenille spread and went inside to phone the undertaker.

The remainder of the morning I could hear her inside the deceased's room, racing the vacuum over the carpeted floor. She threw open his two window sashes to the ceiling. Overhead, the garret was alive with nervous prancing. Lysol fumes wafted throughout the second floor landing. I opened my door a crack and saw Mrs. Vautier scrubbing down his walls with the mixture.

Ostrovsky and I both, at her urging, had to step inside the available tenancy to detect if we could smell Mr. Dobbs. Neither of us could. I, however, winced at the malodorous scent of hardened grease still emanating from iron skillets Ostrovsky stored under his bed. Except for the cadaver and a new chenille spread, this one a cheery yellow, the room looked exactly as it had when the shop teacher flung open its door. Even the double-curved crown felt hat still rested on the chiffonier.

Later that afternoon, a limousine pulled up under my window. Two white-gloved men in dark suits and chauffeur's caps with patent-leather brims carried a black rubber bag with natty Mr. Dobbs inside, and dropped him on the back seat's floorboards.

Just as the mortician assistants sped off, there was a knock on my door.

"Yes?" I answered, thinking surely it was Ostrovsky, wanting to palaver about the vicissitudes of life. Or death. When Mrs. Vautier answered.

"Mr. Daugherty?"

I opened the door. She stood there with a curious smile on her face. Her hands were behind her back. "I want to thank you for helping me take care of that little problem this morning," she said.

"Oh, it was nothing," I said.

The attic peripatetic had settled down.

"I've seen you get dressed on Sunday mornings to go for a walk. You look quite handsome, you know?"

"Oh, thank you," I said, slightly embarrassed.

"Only one thing you are missing, Mr. Daugherty."

"What's that?" I asked.

"This," she said, proffering Mr. Dobbs' steamed fedora with its saffron puggaree, as if it were a fresh pie.

MECHANIC

I miss Betsy.

She knew how to repair cars, hang doors, and finish cement. She enjoyed barroom banter, salacious jokes, and pitching softball. Allison's father admired her, too. Virtually incompetent with his hands, he worked with his head. He didn't like to get dirty; she did, happiest when her face and clothes were smudged with axle grease. He'd have a martini at sundown; she'd open a beer. An unlikely pair sitting next to each other on the western deck, watching darkness descend into the Cape's scrub oak and tortured pine.

The incident occurred when she handed me a turkey baster.

During extended family get-togethers for Thanksgiving or Passover, following the meal, Betsy and I customarily wound up in the kitchen. Unlike the rest, we'd both come from a working class background and found it less stressful to chat while being occupied with some task. The discussion around the table in the dining room generally concerned itself with more abstract matters, like politics, for instance.

Allison and she (they'd been "married" two years) had bought a flaming red Mustang convertible, and Betsy was rebuilding its engine. She'd become interested in automobile mechanics, having watched her father work on the logging truck he owned. I found it fascinating that one of these two women who took the convertible, top down, to soirées in Provincetown, knew more about what made a car go than most men.

So we'd open a six-pack and do the dishes. She washed. I dried. We'd swap bawdy jokes and commiserate about her alcoholic father and my vinous mother—and the Mustang.

"Are the men in your shop taking you seriously yet?" (During the week she worked as a mechanic in a Toyota dealership north of Boston.)

"Oh, yes. Once they found out I could tear an engine apart blindfolded, it was no standoff. Also, I can be just as foul-mouthed as any of them. Men. That's all I've known, for Chissake—six brothers and an old man."

"Your mother didn't have a chance?"

"Dragging on her tits, me and all of her boys. Even the old man. Jesus, she just might as well crawled around on the floor. Like one of those Puerto Rican low-hung street buggies. You dig?"

That's when she handed me the baster.

"Buddy, can we talk?"

"Well, sure, but isn't that what we've been doing?"

"We've been bullshitting like they're doing around the table. I mean real talk."

"Shoot."

"It's about making choices."

"Uh-huh."

"Dammit, I knew it was coming. You don't know what the hell it is, but that it will by Christ show up on your doorstep one morning?"

"I do."

She grabbed the baster. "Gimme that goddamn thing. I don't want to even think about it." The soapsuds dripping off her rugged hands, she motioned that I close the kitchen door.

"What is it, Betsy?"

"Allison," she said.

Two years earlier family and friends gathered in the cottage garden alongside Allison's parents' summer Cape home for a "commitment ceremony." The announcements we all received never mentioned the word *marriage*. Wooden folding chairs were set up under the towering hemlocks, and at the edge of the garden facing away from the ocean stood a makeshift altar draped with a Hermes scarf. A goblet painted gold sat next to a decanter of rosé wine, and behind the altar—a woman pastor dressed in white chiffon and white silk heels. Allison's brother's Fender keyboard and amplifier were hooked up to orange cords snaking through the sand. While the assembled awaited the bride and groom to exit the summer house, Jeremiah played arpeggios with the organ button depressed.

Betsy's father sported a powder blue tuxedo, the same vintage as the '52 Cadillac he and her mother had driven down from Maine. She was stoically attired in a cotton shirtwaist patterned with forget-me-nots. They sat alongside Allison's parents, who were dressed like the university professors they were. When the pastor raised the goblet, Jeremiah laid into the doxology.

I was used to seeing Betsy in coveralls and a sweatshirt with a Chicago Bulls logo. The local Mr. Tux shop had outfitted her in its standard number with a cummerbund, bow tie and zipper fly. She looked like Harpo Marx exiting the garage. As if they'd been shellacked, her lapels reflected the early afternoon sun. Allison wore a white organza ball gown and held a nosegay of calla lilies. Betsy's boutonniere was a lily of the valley sprig.

"Will you take this bride . . . through sickness and in health." From beginning to end—an off-the-shelf service. There was no child ring bearer. At the appointed moment, one of Betsy's friends stood and lifted it out of her alligator purse. The lovers sealed the occasion with an impassioned embrace, I thought, and memorialized the occasion by planting a rose of Sharon tree. Betsy dug the hole.

Following the ceremony, several of the bridal pair's friends coalesced to offer a toast. Allison's father stood on the edge of their knot and hoisted his goblet of champagne, along with theirs. The toaster bristled. "It's a women's only affair," she sniffed. As if an ominous wind gusted in off the Atlantic. Jeremiah ceased doodling "My Foolish Heart."

Betsy stepped forward and wrapped her beefy arms about her father-in-law. "If the old man doesn't drink to our happiness, goddamn it, neither do I."

The straights and gays relaxed, and soon downed several liters of champagne in rapid succession. Betsy drove the red convertible off to Provincetown with high heels of various shades—and her rented brogues—strung to the back bumper. A bed sheet taped to the trunk announced "Newlyweds."

Allison leaned on the Mustang's *do-re-me* horn.

Betsy waved the turkey baster in front of me like a baton. "Allison wants to have a baby, Buddy."

"Oh, Jesus," I said.

"My sentiments, exactly. I'm too old to be a parent. I don't particularly take to kids. Had to put up with enough from my brothers. Cleaning their diapers and watching after them. I love Allison. Christ knows I do. I stopped beating the path to the bars once we got serious. We do wonderful things together. We're good in bed. We're damn kind to each other. Jesus, we're just about to take a trip to Nevada to visit all the casinos in Las Vegas. We'll have a hell of a time, and I don't want to have to begin worrying about some goddamn shit machine."

She was drumming the baster on the Formica table.

After fathering several children of my own, I felt worn out, too.

"It sounds heartless of me, don't it, Buddy?"

"Oh, Jesus, no," I said.

"Look at my mother. What's left of her? All on the bones of my brothers and me."

"You can't talk Allison out of it?"

"She's the bride, right? Picking out nursery wallpaper, for Chrissake. I come home from the shop covered with gunk and grit, looking like my old man after a day in the woods, and she's sitting at the kitchen table with the pattern books. 'Do you like the one with calliopes, Betsy?' Me, I just want to take off my shoes, eat meat, mashed potatoes n' gravy, and read the newspaper."

We both laughed.

"Funny isn't it?"

"But I understand," I said.

"Buddy . . ."

"Yes?"

"I've got no choice."

"You mean to have the baby?"

"It's only natural."

"How do you do that?"

"We've been doing some checking."

"Uh-huh."

"The sperm thing. There are agencies, you know."

"This is all new territory for me, Betsy."

"Like the wallpaper, the bassinet and the crib . . . Allison's re-searched that, too."

"And?"

"It ain't working out the way we want it to."

"Why?"

"I mean it ain't my man oil, you dig?"

"I get that part. So?"

"Where *do* we get it, and how can *we* be sure?"

"You mean the shooter?"

"Yeah," she said.

"I've read where some gay men contribute their sperm to lesbians who want to conceive."

Betsy shook her head disdainfully.

"Why?" I said.

"Paternal rights."

I wasn't getting it.

"Allison has the kid by, say, Harry Potter's seed. It's all antiseptic and politically correct in the beginning. Little Jennifer arrives, and she is a darling. Allison's ecstatic, her whole family's ecstatic . . . and, bingo, so is Harry Potter. He's got rights, too. No damn way, Buddy. We don't want any man staking a claim to our kid."

"So that's out."

"Completely."

"What are your other options?"

"Sperm bank."

"And?"

"They give you this catalog. Air-brushed photographs with the vital statistics of willing male donors. How well each one did on his SATs, if he plays the trumpet, any inherited diseases, and his IQ—if he has any." She shrugged unenthusiastically.

"What's the catch?"

"They're all fucking five foot eight, balding, and in med school."

The noise at the dining room table had turned raucous.

"We went through the catalog twice. I was more interested in the wallpaper."

"I don't even know how the process is done," I said.

"Simple." She wielded the baster before my face.

"You're shitting me."

Betsy shoved it into the turkey's carcass, squeezed the yellow bulb . . . "Now we wait."

"And if it doesn't take?"

"Go on the gizm trail once again. And . . ." Again she thrust it into the carcass. "You men are so lucky."

I could taste her bitterness. We walked back to the now cold and scummy sink water to finish up. It was quiet for the first few pans. There was prolonged laughter in the dining room, about what we weren't certain. Soon the home-baked pies would be set out. Allison's father would be calling for dessert any minute.

"Buddy?"

"What is it?"

"You're educated, and that's important to Allison. But you're real people, too, which is damn important to me. I don't want any kid of mine not to have some sludge in its veins. It needn't be alcohol like my old man or your old lady's got running through theirs . . . but I want her to know what it feels like when she's lying under a chassis and a damn oil pan begins raining black gold across her pretty white face and coloring her hair; it ain't cow piss, Buddy. But it ain't dirt, either."

She was becoming lachrymose.

"Allison's never had to worry where her next dollar was coming from. She ain't had to consider how she might have to take something that didn't belong to her so her brothers could eat."

A flush of red had begin to rise up her neckline.

"I don't give a shit if our kid grows up to listen to Bach or Mozart, or plays the piano like Liberace—screw all that. But it's important to Allison that our kid be educated and not ignorant like his . . ." she hesitated. "Who the fuck am I, Buddy? *Does Allison sleep with me because I'm uncultivated? Because I got graphite moons under my fingernails? Because my tits perspire gasoline when we're wrapped around each other in bed*? I sure as hell ain't like those people sitting in the next room. *You ain't either, Buddy.*" Betsy was tapping the turkey baster against her temple. *"For them, life is all up here.* You get what I'm telling you?"

Of course I was.

"Allison's father sits for hours working out equations on his computer. Yet, when the old professor's crapper goes blank, and the shit threatens to waterfall its porcelain rim—he don't call Einstein. 'Betsy!' he screams. 'Betsy, come here quick!'"

Christ, if someone of the family had come into the kitchen, I don't know what they might have thought: we were in a lover's clutch. Like two brothers hugging, or two sisters, maybe.

She drew away.

"Buddy, we want you to be its father."

Strange how we had reached this fork in the road. I mean humanity's. The complex irony so convoluted it would never be satisfactorily unscrambled. In my mind flashed pictures of Betsy standing in that cheap tuxedo looking blissfully happy that day. Now burdened with the problems of parenthood. Me, the husband of Allison's stepsister, and father many times over.

"Are you asking me to dance, Betsy?"

"Allison and me."

"You're bright like her, dumb like me—and since you got nearly a half-dozen under your belt—you're too damn tired to want to take ours to the ball game or play tea. Whadaya say, Buddy?"

"I've had a vasectomy."

SCATOLOGY

My father took me to the New York World's Fair in 1939. I was five years old. Instead of traveling back in time, he and I journeyed forward on conveyor belts through a silver sphere alongside an obelisk, looking down upon the future. Less than a decade later I saw it again in Levittown.

That midnight train ride across Pennsylvania to the fair wasn't so much to show me what the future held as it was to display his impatience with the past. Father's wingtips and wide-brimmed felt hats, for instance. On New Year's Day he'd give away suits because their lapels were either too ostentatious or too narrow (they vacillated like Cadillac fins). In the summertime our old Dodge sedan he'd have repainted and delegate me to whitewall its tires.

"The ballpoints write under water," he crowed, handing my brother and me Parker pen and pencil sets for graduation. A mahogany bookcase containing the "updated annually" Encyclopedia Americana gathered dust alongside our unused parlor piano. And under the Christmas tree each year—cellophane-boxed shirt and tie combinations with matching cuff links he'd seen advertised by Van Heusen in a recent *Esquire*. Even when we were ten and twelve years old.

I began seeing the connection to brand merchandising and his penchant for staying alive. Hart Schaffner & Marx suits, London Fog coats, Haggar slacks. "Only the best, boys." Jockey shorts were OK in our sock and underwear drawer; Fruit of the Loom would have been frowned upon. Following church services, one of my mother's acquaintances would invariably exclaim:

"Oh, Estelle, what fine little men you have here."

We were little men. In our closets hung little men's suits. All purchased at his haberdashery that catered to the well-off of our town. (Except he bought ours on credit.)

By high school I began to realize there was some connection in my father's mind between brand names and tourist attractions. As he wheedled we wear Arrow shirts, Florsheim shoes, and Dobbs hats, so, too, he insisted we visit the Statue of Liberty, Niagara Falls, the Indy 500 and the Kentucky Derby.

On my sixteenth birthday he took me to New York City. When the cab driver picked us up at Grand Central, Father said, "Times Square."

"And where to there, sir?"

"The Astor."

He'd listened to Sammy Kaye's radio broadcasts from its Stardust Roof. On that trip, separated from him for several hours one evening, I found my way into a 52nd Street jazz club. The Birdland marquee advertised Charlie Parker and Bud Powell.

"Pap, tonight I heard the most incredible music I've ever listened to. Sammy Kaye and Guy Lombardo don't play like these cats. Can't we go back there tomorrow night?"

But we had to see the sights—Greenwich Village and the men-girlie shows, walk the Bowery. Radio City Music Hall and the Rockettes. "And we must get dressed up for that date," he said. He'd wear his Bostonians he'd purchased on sale earlier in the day. I wore a McGregor shirt and sport coat.

Mother was more interested in making what little money he brought into the house last longer, otherwise our house would have been stuffed with Westinghouse appliances. But on the few occasions the couple went out in public, she basked in his brand-name presence.

Early on I sensed it was all kind of sad. Visiting the Empire State Building was his pilgrimage to Lourdes. Except no miracle ever occurred. One empty experience after another. Like the Arrow shirts. He'd boast to his friends or the bartender:

"Just returned from New York City. Took the Staten Island Ferry. Saw the Copper Lady. Went to the Copacabana and the Village. The Rockettes kicked up one helluvan Easter show."

"Yeah?" the bartender would respond. "Never been there. But I do watch Macy's Thanksgiving Parade every year."

"Took my boy Ben there, too. Had chop suey in Chinatown. We did it all." Then he'd order another double Seagrams with a beer chaser.

As I grew older, I had a recurring dream in which I saw him strolling through our deserted town, pasted over by advertising slogans and tourist brochures. These icons of our culture—his motor oil for conversations. But I also saw something deeper.

I saw him naked.

How dapper he always looked. How the patrons would look up from their drinks when he entered the bar. "Here comes Kelman. Looks like the mannequin stepped right out of Levine's Men's Wear window, 'eh, Bud?"

How he insisted my brother and I do the same. Tiny men placards for brand names that had a greater cachet than Sears & Roebuck, Montgomery Ward, or JC Penney's.

"Nothing but the best, boys. It's how people judge you."

I judged him when he was stripped, spitting up his guts on a Saturday evening after a day at the saloon; or when he soiled himself—and crawled around on all fours in his Hickey Freeman threads, thinking he was going to die he was so drunken sick.

The brands didn't succor him through these existential moments. The Copper Lady, the Bowery, Chinatown, Times Square, Coney Island, and the Staten Island Ferry all fell short in his latter days when he sat staring at the walls, wrapped in a Montgomery Ward flannel night coat—Apache design—with a cloth belt. Surely wondering what in God's name it had all added up to.

He couldn't even give away the Arrow Shirts that were yellowing at the collar. Or the Florsheim shoes, now a decade out of style—Christ, he needed only one pair if they were going to display him . . . but he insisted that nobody do that.

"You got to promise, sons."

Was he afraid his weeds would be out of style? That one of us might pick out the wrong shirt and tie combination if we didn't cremate him? That the lapels on his suit jacket looked like dragonfly wings? The hair tonic didn't smell like Vitalis? Maybe some drinking buddy would stick a chintzy replica of the Empire State Building in the bier alongside him?

Oh, I could see the change coming. The last few years of his life he was no longer the sartorial signboard. He still put up the front, but it didn't have the old conviction. I knew this for certain when he came to visit me in his last year.

I picked him up at Logan airport. He shuffled down a long corridor, last in line. A flight attendant alongside, carting his Samsonite luggage of an earlier vintage. Normally any woman that close he'd have engaged in animated conversation. Instead, he concentrated on getting to the exit gate, catching his breath every dozen steps.

"Pap, you look exhausted."

"Too much," he said. "I can't take it like I used to."

"Let's sit down."

"If I stop, I won't be able to get started again. Where's your car?"

On the journey to my house, he was silent. Earlier times he'd of been palavering about whom he had met on the plane. A stranger from Arizona, or Montana perhaps, insisting he visit. Then he'd remember a trip we'd once taken across the States. "Don't you remember, Ben? The Hoover Dam. Mount Rushmore?"

But the spring in the windup mouse was at its last coil. When we walked into my house, he asked for a drink. I placed a bottle of unopened Seagrams on the kitchen table. He wanted me to help him take off his suit coat, his tie, assist him with his shoes. He found it difficult to bend over. "Having trouble breathing," he complained.

I poured a water glass half full of whiskey. He took a long drink, then wet-dog shuddered.

"I feel dirty," he said. "Sweaty from sitting in those cramped airplane seats. I want to wash off."

"Wash your face?" I asked.

"No, my body. I want to take a shower."

Back home we had a bathtub that'd lost its porcelain finish in spots from being scoured black.

"There's a shower in the cellar. It's how we bathe," I said.

He took another drink and walked down the cellar steps.

Momentarily he called me down. "What is it, Pap?"

He stood outside the shower door, looking bewildered. I'd never seen him in this condition. Always telling me and my brother what to do. "Buy the best, sons."

"Are you alright, Pap?"

"Will you help me?"

I walked over and he held his arms out, gesturing I undress him. I took his shirt off and draped it over a chair under the cellar window. A late afternoon slant of sun cut a shard across the concrete floor. The metal shower stall's plastic curtain was pulled to one side with a swag. I sat him down in the old kitchen chair, its layers of paint alligatoring, unfastened his Hickok belt and undid his pants' zipper. He lifted one leg and then another as I slid them loose and folded them on their crease, placing them on a hanger. I removed his black rayon ankle socks.

"Will you get the water ready, Son? Not too hot. Just tepid."

I turned my back to him and twisted the shower faucet, causing the water to run lukewarm. When I turned back, he was standing there nude, handing me his Jockey shorts. They looked to me as if this was their first wear.

"Ben, throw these away for me, please."

I stared at him.

"Where's the trash?" he said.

"What's wrong with them, Pap?"

"They have a stain on them, Son."

"So, we throw them in the wash."

"No," he insisted. "I buy a three-pack once a week."

My sister stopped at the house once a week to pick up his laundry and would return what she'd laundered the following day.

"What are you talking about?" I said.

"The mud stains, Son. Much simpler for me to toss them in the rubbish than to listen to her ranting about "shitty underwear.""

As he stood motionless behind the orange-fish curtain, I stared at the thumbprint umber stain on the fleece-white Jockey shorts. Christ, it's *his* earth, I thought. In weeks, perhaps days, this is all I will have left of him. Like blood it appeared to me. And balling up the Y-fronts, I stuffed them into my face and fucking cried.

Yeah, I'll throw them away, I thought. Fuck yeah. Where? In the ocean? The sky? Where do you want me to toss them, God? Onto the face of the Copper Lady? Under the Brooklyn Bridge? How about I scrub them white with sand from Jones' Beach, or run them twice through the lobby of the Waldorf Astoria? Can I remove the stain if I rinse them in a Mint Julep at the Kentucky Derby? Maybe I camouflage the brown earth, his brown earth, with sauce from Mama Leone's? Or holy water from Saint Patrick's Cathedral?

And when the plastic shower curtain parted, he stood white as albumen.

"Will you run upstairs and get me that drink I haven't finished, Son?"

"In a minute, Pap. First let's dry you off."

I walked toward him and held him to me. Christ, so tight. I wanted my energy to seep into his trembling body.

He didn't resist. One in an Arrow shirt, Levis, and Sperry boat shoes. The other buck naked.

Watching half light filter through the foundation window.

A pungent odor of earth rising off the concrete floor.

THE NEWS FROM HEAVEN

I know Jeremiah didn't expect it. Probably hadn't crossed his mind since he was a kid. We never talked about it, even then. Except the day David McKensey slipped into the pool of acid wash runoff at Blair Strip Steel. A cortege of freshly-washed family sedans paraded down our street that morning. I remember Jeremiah didn't want to go to Castleview with the rest of us. Actually, I was curious. My first experience with somebody I knew leaving this world and never returning . . . so they said. Hard to believe that when you are a kid. I wanted to see how they made sure he wasn't coming back, how deep they were going to drop him into the earth. I'd seen Houdini have his helpers stuff him into a milk can, cinch it up with big chains and locks, then toss him into the water.

They'd closed little David in a copper casket and were about to drop it into the ground deeper than a grown man could climb out if he had no ladder. Didn't appear they were giving him much of a chance. But I wasn't convinced like the rest of them that one day he wasn't going to show up on one of our front porches. And did we have an extra orange we could spare.

Just like they told me my dog, Shadow, had gone away. Nobody was too happy the day I found him following me home. Nearly three miles I kept telling him "Get away!" but he wasn't about to turn back. Must've come from somebody in the circus. I got to imagining he belonged to the freak I saw drive sixteen-penny nails in his feet and dip cattails into kerosene, ignite them, and stick them into his mouth—for the cur wasn't afraid of anything. Cars, nothing. I'd get mean with him, knowing it wouldn't be easy to keep him in our house . . . but to no effect. Right on my heels.

Often I'd look out the classroom window seeing him lying in the grass, probably as bored as I was. Our day didn't begin until school was out. He slept beside my bed, too. But they didn't want him. Tried to find any excuse for me to get rid of him. I knew if I couldn't come up with one, they would. So the day I came home from school and told Ma that Shadow wasn't waiting for me, she confided that Father had taken Shadow for a ride.

"A ride where, Ma?"

"A ride in the country, Westley. Out to a farm where there's lots of room, acres and acres of room, and all sort of livestock. Cows, pigs, chickens, turkeys, and children like you—lots of them. Think of the fun Shadow will have. He won't have to be cooped up here in the house, or waiting outside all alone while you are spending your day in school. He can help herd the cows into the barn at night. Sleep in the hayloft and keep the fox out of the chicken roost."

"Whose farm is this that Pa took Shadow to, Mom?"

"Some friend of a friend of his at the plant."

"How far away is it?"

"Oh far, very far, your father said. I don't expect him home 'til dark."

I knew down in my heart how far. About as far as heaven is from the earth. Old Shadow was never coming back. It was dog's heaven what she was describing. Sounded just the sort of place Shadow would speak of retiring to if he could dream like us. Probably in a stream somewhere now stiller than a stone, all balled up in a burlap sack with a rope wound tight about its opening.

Near a week later I was walking home from school and Ned Jenkins, my friend—I can see him running toward me from down by Potter's grocery store. He's hollering, "Westley, hey, Westley! C'mere, quick!"

And I go running to him, when he yells he thinks Shadow's lying down on the curb in front of Potter's.

"Is he dead?" I cried.

"It don't look like he's dead. Just dead tired. He's lying there panting and keeping his eye on me. I know it's him, Westley."

We both ran to the bottom of the street, and yessir, there was old Shadow with a brown spot and black spot on his white coat, panting for dear life.

"Run into Potter's and get a pan of water, Ned. Shadow's dying of thirst."

I bent over him, and the animal licked my face. His tongue was dry as composition paper, but the tail began beating against the granite curb. "Oh, Shadow, you've come home. You and Houdini. I knew it. I promise I'll never believe them again. Jesus, I thought you were gone for good."

Ned held the pan of water up to his snout, and as Shadow lapped up the cool liquid, I scooped handfuls onto his head and rubbed his dusty eyes. I examined his paws. They were all bloody, as if he'd been crossing a hot macadam road back from wherever dog heaven or hereafter is. Like scabs, the tar roads . . . the hundreds of miles that he'd run coming back to me . . . must have pulled the pads off his feet, leaving the fiery, oozing mess.

When Shadow walked into the house with me, it was like Ma saw a ghost. Up to then she always had an answer for everything. Shadow had come back from the dead, traveled for days from that bullshit farm in the sky that they tried to feed me, and there he was walking up to her and licking her legs.

Ma was speechless. Finally she said, "Your father will be surprised."

I could keep Shadow now. Nobody in their right mind would dare toy with the gods. You might return something twice to a store. But you wouldn't send a dog back to the celestial dog farm for fear more than one would come home the second time.

• • •

I figured it wasn't no different with my brother, Jeremiah. I got the call about noontime. It was from his wife, May.

"Westley, Jeremiah's gone."

"Gone where?" I said.

"He was helping a neighbor build a deck on his house. Came home for lunch half hour ago. Opened the screen door into the kitchen, looked at me kind of strange. 'What's wrong, honey?' I say. 'I'm feeling sick to my stomach all of sudden,' he says. I could see it, Westley. He got ghost-white, and I drop a plate on the floor. By then he'd collapsed. 'Jeremiah, speak to me! What's ailing you?' But he's looking right through me, Westley. As if somebody were standing behind us—he nodded like you do in church when the preacher says something you know is right and you just haven't wanted to admit it to yourself?"

She was going on and on. "Jesus Christ, May, is my brother dead?"

"He is," she sobbed. "What are the children and I ever going to do without him?"

Then I started bawling. I had a woodlot up in Maine, and Saturday nights, late when our women were in bed, our kids were sound asleep, he and I'd get on the telephone, hundreds of miles apart, open a six-pack, and discuss just where among the hemlock we were going to situate the two cabins whose logs we'd already peeled and notched inside our heads.

Next Saturday night we'd palaver about the '46 Indian motorcycle he'd bought and kept stored in his garage for the day we could get together and rebuild it.

Just a question of how soon.

Now here this ups and happens. Like Shadow, my brother's been hauled off to heaven, the preacher solicitously told me. "It's where he is for certain, Westley. Weren't no better man than Jeremiah Daugherty on this old earth. He's up there waiting for you all to join him." He lived in Virginia when he left us. I wondered if I'd meet him in a Virginia heaven or in our Pennsylvania heaven.

Of course the hardest it hit anybody beside May were Mom and Pap. (Jeremiah's son dropped a sixteen-oz. hammer into his father's casket, suggesting his respect for the doctrine of earthly departure.) May didn't want to test the hearts of either of our parents, so she phoned over to Rudy in Harmony to get the news to them. Rudy's an alcoholic and Jeremiah's and my brother-in-law. By noontime he gets excessively maudlin over even the most trivial matters. Well, he rushes up to the house and gathers Mom and Pap into the living room.

"What is it, Rudy?" they importune. "Why are you doing this?"

"Just trust me. Pap, you sit over there. Here, Mom, you sit right down next to me on the sofa." Mother's arthritic, so it takes her some time to bend down and get seated. Pap has cataracts and feels his way into the overstuffed chair.

"Well, I've got some bad news to share with you."

Rudy is trying to be brave about this, but starts blubbering and grabs onto Mother like he were her son. Pap gets alarmed and stares at Ma. "What ain't you telling her and me, Rudy?" Rudy is bawling so loud, Pap has to get cross with him . . . to break him out of the jag. Pap had experience with this kind of thing.

"Rudy, now goddamn it, straighten up! Why did you come up here? What is it Mother and me should know?"

"Jeremiah fell over in his kitchen dead this very noon," he sobbed.

It was like lightning leapt off the telephone pole outside our house and jumped right into the living room. Ma dropped onto the sofa. Pap, he got suddenly cold and motionless, staring at the Vitrone's house across the street like he was trying to pierce through their drapes that were always closed.

Rudy stood and staggered toward the door. A low moan began to build in Mother's breast. As it rose, so did she. Ma crawled into Pap's lap, clutching him for dear life. He returned the embrace, but it was limpid. Soon the two of them mewled. A kind of old-folks we-shouldn't-have-to-do-it dirge for having to bury their youngest son—still the blue sky in her eyes. Rudy got in his car and hurried off to a saloon.

Well, Jeremiah and I hadn't made our plans lightly. I was convinced that late one afternoon somebody was going to be phoning me up saying they saw my brother. "I know it's him . . . lying alongside a curb," maybe not in Harmony, but some town like Ashtabula or Cincinnati, Ohio, lying there, panting with a dry tongue and waiting for me to bring the water. Not the water of tears. Been enough of that.

And I'd carry it, no matter how many miles or days I'd have to travel, I'd have a sack of it cooling on my back like the water bags of burlap used to hang off chromium car bumpers, thirst quenching, as families headed west, motoring across Arizona and the hot sands of New Mexico. When I'd come upon him resting there near naked in the gutter, I'd stoop over and kiss his damp forehead, take his dry tongue, dry as the parchment of his phony death certificate where the doctor lied about the cardial infarction, dip it into my water bag and watch the light return to his eyes.

"Remember, the Indian in your garage?" I'd say. "Well, I fired her up this morning. And she runs good as new."

Then I heard him gurgle, not the catarrh of death creeping up in his throat, but the phlegm of life about to rise out of his lungs, clearing it for new oxygen. And I took his feet in my hands, his bloody feet that he ran all the way back from Hell on, and they were on fire. Bloody fire. And I licked them with my wet tongue. Licked the fire right off them. Jesus, they were hot and salty. Salty as cur's weep wetting us both.

"Fuck the dog farm in the sky!" I yelled. "Fuck the dog farm in heaven, Jeremiah. You've come home. My brother. My sweet fucking shadow. Don't ever leave me again."

SOIL

Leonard's father, brother Felix, and he vowed early on to get out of
town. His mother and sisters had no such ambition. "Perfectly fine
for us under the willow tree in our backyard."

"We want Gotham instead," the men said.

Mr. Hart never made it. Following a deathbed request, Leonard took the bus to Geneva-on-the-Lake, Ohio, where the family
spent one week each summer, walked to the water's edge, said a
brief prayer, and shook his father free of the black funerary urn.

It was empty.

Mrs. Hart and Leonard's sisters had salted him under the willow tree.

Even more determined to escape Hebron—"You'll perish here,"
Mr. Hart prophesied—Felix borrowed his father's sedan one Sunday afternoon. Its carburetor burst into flames on a country road,
as did Felix, who trotted across a wheat field, dripping fire. "That's
one way of getting out," Leonard mused.

They sprinkled young Felix under the willow tree, too.

A summer night preceding his senior year in high school, Leonard
waited until his sisters and mother were sound asleep before waltz-
ing out of the house. His Schwinn bicycle stationed against the willow tree. Carrying only a change of clothes in a pillowcase, he knelt.
"Pap, Felix—I'll come home for you someday. Keep the faith." He
embraced the tree.

Anguishing over his departure, Mrs. Hart traveled to nearby towns on weekends and spoke to merchants in an effort to track down her son. A neighbor, two years after the incident, swore she saw him standing on his head atop a golden palomino in a Mills Brothers circus over in Meadville. That same week, another said her daughter had seen him playing drums in a cocktail lounge at Conneaut Lake Park.

Leonard, over time, was spotted singing with Stan Kenton's band in Cleveland's Starlight Ballroom; as an extra in *From Here To Eternity*; on a Pennzoil racing team at the Indianapolis 500. Then one Christmas Eve, the local butcher told Mrs. Hart her son was a missionary in Havana, Cuba.

"How are you sure, Mr. Albertini?"

"Che Guevara and the Holy Mother appeared to me in my dreams last night. It's Leonard—the priest masquerading as a revolutionary."

But Leonard Hart was holed up in a single room tenancy on 114th Street in Manhattan, one block off Broadway and near Columbia University. He worked replenishing shelves in a Times Square bookstore, and to make ends meet, periodically sold his blood—five dollars for the first pint, seven dollars thereafter. Only once had he encountered someone he knew from Hebron—Gertrude Eckstrom, his high school drama coach. Engrossed in reading a copy of *Billboard*, she took a seat opposite him at the Horn and Hardart Automat. Leonard fled, leaving his soup and Parker House rolls untouched.

His attire he acquired at a Goodwill thrift shop on East 57th Street. Preferring Brooks Brothers suits, he owned one chalk-striped blue serge and a cocoa-brown three-piece worsted. His recycled shoes were cordovan and a vintage forties camel hair topcoat he saved for special occasions. The closet in his SRO was not much larger than a broom stand.

"At least I've made it to Manhattan," he thought, and did avail himself of its art museums, especially the Frick, the public library reading room on 42nd Street, and an occasional subway ride to Greenwich Village. There he'd sit in the corner of the White Horse

Tavern and read Thomas Wolfe, the chesterfield draped over an empty cafe chair.

When Columbia was in session, Leonard attended the university's Y.W.C.A. Saturday night socials sponsored for its unattached women. A shot of Scotch at the West End Bar on Broadway (the ghosts of Merton, Ginsberg, Kerouac and Lucien Carr pettifogged in the corner booth) helped gel his courage to approach a stranger. To an uncritical eye, Leonard Hart in the blue-serge and bluchers looked as if he might be the scion of an upper-class family, residents of the Mystic coastline.

The evening he introduced himself to Emma Thomas, a graduate student in English Literature, he fully understood why his father had insisted he escape Hebron. She waxed of the "Faerie Queen" in the rose of moonlight illuminating the hall's Palladian window, her moth-dust neck and shoulders draped by a black *crepe de chine* scarf. After several sets, she grew less intense and announced she actually was Miss Cunegund, and would he teach her the steps to the Totentranz?

"Emma, will I really see you next Saturday?" he said.

"Yes," she teased. "We'll dance again."

That evening, he wore the brown worsted with a vest and a yellow shirt, and a red silk tie embroidered with miniature Perriots he'd purchased that afternoon. From a street vendor, he'd bought a gardenia that Emma might pin in her auburn hair—wiry, cropped close to her oval head, and emitting the scent of camomile. She wore a tea-length indigo velvet dress scooped at the bodice. Her shoes were claret Mary-Janes.

"What do you do, Leonard?" she asked.

"I act," he said.

Midway through the dance, Emma rested her head upon his shoulder. The pair cast no shadows in the Palladian rose. *But how can I ask her back to my room? The stage curtain would rise,* he anguished.

"Where do you stay, Emma?"

"The menopause hotel."

He glanced awkwardly at his shoes.

"Graduate woman's flat," she said. "Male callers forbidden."

"No such restrictions in my dormitory," he replied.

As they climbed up five flights of steps to his room, Emma and he suddenly became engrossed in a dumb show. Especially fond of Eugene Ionesco's writing, Leonard began ushering imaginary guests in the French playwright's drama "The Chairs" into their seats; Emma, amused by his comic antics, followed suit. They danced up, then part way back down, the Riverside Suites staircase . . . exhorting the hotel's male occupants to accompany them into Hart's room.

"A masque and drinks in room 505!" Emma cried.

"The Faerie Queen unveils Miss Cunegund!" he advertised.

At the fifth landing, exhausted as if after coitus, silly, and still alone—Leonard could barely fit the key in the lock. He shouldered the door open.

Emma paled.

A metal cot dressed by an olive drab blanket and a bureau of drawers sat jammed against each other. He had to walk sideways to access his closet. A singular overhead light tube illuminated manuscript wallpaper, yellowed and brittle. An area of the wall covering alongside Leonard's bed had worn through to mottled plaster. In bold red script, he—or a stranger—had scratched: *Jesus wept. Voltaire smiled.* A squeezed tube of Ipana toothpaste, a bottle of Vaseline Hair Tonic, and a mute wind-up clock sat atop the metal bureau.

"Where do you act?" Emma inquired enigmatically, absently covering her head with the chiffon scarf. As if he'd never inhaled her camomile, shuddered her first breath upon his neck—and now denied witnessing her "yes" congeal the cold fluorescent light as he undraped the alba-skinned, the faerie russet-haired, Miss Cunegund.

Leonard switched off the overhead fixture, hoping to douse the houselights. Miss Thomas nervously shifted at the threshold. "It's getting late," she said.

"I'll walk you back to your hotel."

"No," she replied, stiffly placing her hands into her coat pockets. "It's not your fault, Mr. Hart."

"Why?" he asked.

"Foolishly we got carried away. We invited too many guests."

He counted her steps. Twenty-five each floor.

The following Saturday, Leonard once again wore the blue serge. But Emma Thomas never showed. Nor the next Saturday, or the one after that. He loitered about the English Department during class hours. On days off he sat for hours in Butler Library, hoping she might reappear.

Gone. As he'd vanished from Hebron. And with her the charm of other men's garments, a stranger's chesterfield coat.

What had she seen when he opened the door to his room?

Mr. Hart and Felix. Emerging out of the yellowed-manuscript walls. The elder wearing a bowler and double-breasted three piece black gabardine, a white shirt buttoned at the collar with no tie, standing barefoot. His son wearing the clothes in which they found him immolated in a wheat field. The right sleeve of the leather jacket burned off at the elbow, the breast charred like a barbecued pig's, the pant legs missing except the crotch and its environs. Fire stays clear of a dying man's watery fear.

Emma saw them.

Standing against the closet wall when Leonard opened the door.

"Hoodwinking Miss Thomas into thinking I'm somebody who I know I am not. '*As it was in the beginning is now and ever shall be.*' Felix and Father cajoling me to return for them . . . Yet, I'm concentrating on suspending Emma's disbelief, willing that she disrobe and absorb the room's cold light into her fiery genitalia and camomile hair—willing she succumb to the cell of male history as I cause her to sing.

"Surely, I'd relax then."

Wearing the chalk-stripe suit and freshly polished cordovans, Leonard took a midnight train ride back across the States to Hebron. The following morning, he knocked at his homestead door.

"Grace?"

No response.

"It's me—Leonard," he said.

Grace let out a cry. "Phyllis! Linda!" The prodigal brother stood in the doorway, looking like a freshly minted fifty-dollar bill.

"You've come home!" the sisters sang, embracing him and each other. They drew their brother into the living room.

"Where's Mother?" Leonard asked.

"You must be hungry," Phyllis said.

They led him into the kitchen, set exactly as he remembered it as a boy. The Formica chromium dinette set, the porcelain sink basin scoured through in spots to its cast iron, the one-light door overlooking the backyard.

The sisters hovered nearby. Grace poured the coffee. "She's gone, Leonard. Nobody knew where to find you. Word had it that you were singing for a dance band out of Cleveland."

"Riding trick horses in a traveling circus," Linda added. "But Mr. Albertini convinced Mother you were a missionary in Cuba."

Leonard smiled.

"Each day she waited for the mail. Never once stopped believing that you were the only one of us whoever made good."

"Is she. . . ?"

Phyllis pointed to the willow tree.

A red bicycle, its spokes and handlebars powdered by rust, cloaked in the radiant perse blue of a winter morning.

AMBUSH

One a.m., the phone rings. I know who it is and don't wish to answer it.

"Which one of the girls is hurt or sick?"

"It's Grace."

"Uh-huh, in the hospital or worse?"

"Worse."

"Can't be worse."

"Believe me."

Grace is the youngest of my three daughters.

"What is it, Beth? Get to the goddamned point."

"I can't handle her."

"Are you saying you want me to step in?" We have had this conversation before. I volunteer to have Grace live with me, but insist if she does, it's until her eighteenth birthday. Beth always objects.

"She's stopped going to school and is out every night running around with twenty-year-olds, and they're no choir boys."

"Where is she now?"

"No idea."

"You understand—I take her, she's under my control and no interference from you? No 'Oh-Grace-you-come-home-to-Mamma' bullshit."

"Agreed."

There was a note of futility in Beth's voice. I lived downtown. She and my daughters lived in the Bronx, the Riverdale section. A half-hour ride this hour of the morning.

Beth sat at the kitchen table when I arrived. "Every night, Lee." She shrugged. "I never know when she's going to show. And something else—she drinks."

Not a surprise. "Drugs?"

"I don't know."

"I'll pick up her clothes and essentials in a day or two. You go to bed."

"We'll both wait."

Divorced six years, Beth and I have run out of things to say to each other. I pulled a chair up alongside the door. She sat over in a dark corner of the living room, smoking. Three-thirty a.m. Grace flounces into the apartment, sees me sitting in the hallway, and lets out a laugh. "Dad, what are you doing here?"

"Leave your coat on."

She takes it off and begins looking about the room for her mother. A fifteen-year-old in a woman's skin dressed like her mother when I first met her in a dance hall back in Ashtabula. Grace, who'd been drinking, is attempting to humor me while insinuating her mother's betrayal.

"What did you call Dad for, Ma?"

Beth slouched farther down into the sofa. I hand Grace her coat.

"Take yours off," she responds. "Nice of you to visit. Little early in the morning though, don't you agree, Ma?" she sneered.

"Put your goddamn coat on, Grace." It's now lying on the floor between us.

"I'm not putting my coat on for you or anybody else." A summer earlier she'd played league softball, and before her attitude had begun to shift, shot-putted at high school.

I grabbed her arm.

"Oh no!" she said.

"Uh-huh . . ." We were on the floor, she struggling to break free of my grip. "You're coming with me, girl. This no-accountability life of yours is all over. Changing of the fucking guard!"

I'd never seriously wrestled with a woman before—let alone my daughter. Grace and I rose and fell several times before she finally succumbed. I'd pinned her arms above her head and straddled her chest. She turned sullenly to Beth . . . who glided nervously back and forth before the picture window.

"Don't touch one goddamn thing of mine! I'll be back tomorrow."

My International Harvester Scout sat under the streetlight. Grace lit up a cigarette as we drove off. So far so good, I thought. Over the six years of separation we'd seen each other at least twice a week. The three girls initially. Then when they grew older, it made more sense to see them individually. So we'd rotate weeks. (Neither Beth nor I had remarried.) My visits with the girls were always phrenetic—a forced "happy hour" that they learned to endure and I couldn't have done without. Until a year ago when they abruptly stopped. Each girl asked separately, "Dad, can't we just visit you on a more casual basis?" They were growing up.

I crossed the Spyten Dyvil bridge and drove onto Westside Drive. Grace hadn't spoken a word until the Dyckman Street exit in the Bronx. "Turn off here!" she ordered.

"But that's not the way downtown."

"Do it!" she cried. And grabbed the steering wheel, forcing us off the road.

"Grace!"

"Trust me."

I exited and pulled the car over to the curb. "What's this all about?"

"I'll tell you later."

She wasn't attempting to jump out of the car, so I dropped it and took Broadway south. Periodically she'd look to either side of the car as vehicles passed, or out the back window to see if we were being followed. In the Fifties she visibly relaxed.

"What's going on, Grace?"

"Nothing now."

"Then?"

"You were about to be ambushed." She lit another cigarette.

"I don't get it."

"We saw your car."

"Who?"

"Me and my friends. 'He's here to take me away,' I told them. 'Get ready.'"

"Is this some kind of story, Grace?"

"They were going to force you off the road down along 125th Street, one of those turn-offs near the river. Then pull me loose. It was all planned."

"And me?"

She didn't respond.

Neither of us spoke to each other until we got to my apartment. At the door, I asked: "These boys you're talking about ambushing me?"

"Yeah?"

"Tell me."

"Ralph's an ex-con out of Wallkill. He ain't been a boy for some time."

She ascended the stairs first. Built just like her mother. I couldn't tell them apart from the rear. The high heels with rhinestone shooting-star clasps, the shimmering pantyhose in the hallway amber light, roan hair that fell to her shoulders—and a scent that any man penned in a cage could never forget.

Alex, my current companion, met us at the door. She took Grace's coat. "Can I fix you some tea?" Grace refused, excused herself for the bathroom. Moments later she crashed on my couch, her coat still on, and fell fast asleep. Over breakfast the next morning I realized she hadn't been in school for months.

"What were you doing?" I asked.

"Hanging out with friends."

"Ralph?"

"Yes."

"Where?"

She lit a cigarette.

"Well, that's all going to change, Grace."

"Yeah, sure," she snorted. "I get it. OK. I don't mind school. I'll go back home and promise I'll attend regularly."

"There is no going back, Grace."

"What do you mean?"

Alex glanced hard at me.

"I'm *not* living with you."

"Uh-huh."

Grace looked at Alex. "*The three of us?*"

Alex nodded her head.

"You mean I am going to school around here?"

"No," I answered. "We're leaving for Maine."

"*Maine!*"

"Tomorrow."

"To do fucking what?"

"Live," Alex said softly.

"In Maine?" Grace jumped up from the table and grabbed her coat. "You think you're taking me away from my friends to live in Maine?"

"What are they going to do, Grace? Ambush folks in Maine—up there they'll blow your head off."

Grace started to laugh maniacally and pace. "This is all a joke." She glared at Alex, who entered our bedroom to return with the suitcases.

"It's beautiful up there this time of year, Grace. It'll do you good, do us all good to get the city out of our systems. It's poisoned us. We'll stop at your house on the way north to pick up warm clothes."

Grace had it in her mind this would all pass. Over the period of separation when any crisis among the siblings would erupt, Beth and I'd get together to formulate some grandiose, well-intentioned plan to smooth things out. We'd set the girls down, explaining how we'd spent hours of soul-searching. How good it was going to be from there on out. The children would dutifully listen—and we all felt better. Like having been released from a prolix church service. Outside the vestibule, the sun illumining the pastor who wishes every parishioner a bountiful week, while inside the organ lobs hosannahs against the empty chapel's walls. Cleansed.

But in a very short period these plans invariably withered. The animus between Beth and me remained unchanged. Grace and her sisters still had to navigate our selfish needs, which by this time they were all adept at.

In her mind, surely it was, "Fuck Maine. So we go up there for a few days. He'll have a change of heart. Mother will call, insisting I return home. Get to a phone and call Ralph. It's cool."

When we stopped to pick up Grace's clothes, her luggage sat packed on the porch. Beth didn't even appear in the window.

Alex and I had rented a house in rural Maine several months earlier. Once a summer residence for a Boston Brahmin, after years of being unoccupied it had fallen into a state of disrepair. In exchange for my carpentry services, his out-of-state relatives cut our rent substantially. Located a mile in on a camp road along the mountainous back side of a lake with one shuttered summer cottage along the way—it couldn't have felt more remote this early November.

We arrived at two in the morning. The moon silvered the lake's icy surface whose far side abutted a one-general-store town. Grace had slept most of the way, resigned to wait Alex and me out by responding indifferently to anything we uttered.

"It's serene here in the summer, Grace." We walked past the boathouse toward the main residence, or "Mountain Lodge" as the local people knew it. "There's a vintage Chris-Craft motorboat lying in a slip inside there, all mahogany and appointed with chromium spotlights. A real beauty you can run the lake at night with."

She climbed the steps ahead of me. At the entryway I inserted the key. "You're going to love this place. It has a winter and summer quarters. Twelve rooms. Your choice. The bedrooms facing the water are the loveliest."

The house had been shut tight for three months—the air inside stale and bone-chilling. Fusty air always penetrates the body deeper than cold, outside air, no matter what the temperature. I immediately set to throwing sticks into the kitchen's wood stove, then lit the console Atlantic wood burner in the winter living quarters. Upstairs the Lodge was heated by warm air rising through filigreed cast-iron registers inset in the downstairs' ceiling. I activated the pump which began drawing water up from the lake. Soon Alex brewed coffee.

We listened to Grace's spike heels drumming the hardwood floors, wandering in and out of the upstairs' chambers. They stopped over the kitchen, the darkest room in the Lodge. It looked out upon a ledge less than six feet from the back of the house that rose vertically for another 150 feet. The "cottage" had been built on a shelf blasted out of the granite rise in the thirties by the merchant who'd amassed his wealth acquiring wool from Northeast sheep farmers, then selling it to the government for World War I uniforms.

Grace's bedroom furniture had all been painted cottage-white: a spool bed, a dresser with an oversized rococo mirror and an arrow-back kitchen chair that sat in the corner. The walls had been freshly painted robin's-egg blue.

Tuesday morning, once we'd taken the chill off the downstairs, I hollered up for Grace to join us at breakfast. She refused. When I knocked on her door, and she didn't respond, I opened it to find her lying under several blankets in the bed, motionless.

"I'm not hungry," she said. It became her refrain for lunch and dinner.

Wednesday, a repeat of Tuesday.

By Thursday morning, Alex had begun to express concern. "She's going to starve herself, Lee. It's how she's going to beat you."

"I don't give up easily," I said.

"You don't understand the will of young women."

"I'm every bit as strong and determined as she is."

"Suppose she continues to refuse food?"

"When she gets hungry enough—she'll give in."

"After a couple of days . . . the pangs of hunger lessen."

"She's got to come downstairs to drink."

"Already beat you on that."

"What do you mean?"

"She's cupping snow off the window sills."

Tuesday it had begun to snow nonstop. I'd spoken to a town select-man about plowing our camp road. "We don't plow out driveways," he said. I told him I had a teenage daughter down by the lake, and he and the town fathers damn well better keep the lane clear or I'd call the State's Department of Education. "What if something happened and we need an ambulance? Am I supposed to swim across the damn lake for help?"

The five-acre body of water looked like a meadow blanketed by snow.

Friday and Saturday Grace still didn't show. Alex found a desktop radio, an ivory Philco model, in one of the summer rooms and set it inside her door. We could hear she'd tuned into a station of top hits coming out of Lewiston. She played it nonstop. Saturday evening when I knocked, there was no answer. I pushed open her door and was surprised to see her standing at the mirror, dressed in the very same clothes she wore the night I picked her up. A black jersey dress that draped provocatively over her breasts and hugged her buttocks. She had hose on and black silk spikes with rhinestone shooting-stars clips on each toebox. While brushing her chestnut hair, she'd obsessively reach down to change the station after the song's first minute or so of play.

I sat on her bed. "Will you join us for dinner? Alex's prepared a tuna casserole, the kind you always enjoyed when your mother made it. She's baked cornbread, too. I guess you already smelled that, huh, Grace?"

She sprayed cologne about her neck and shoulders.

"We're missing your company, you know? It's easy to get lonely up here. People have to stick together to get through the long winters. If you'd come downstairs to look out across the lake, or down the path toward our car, you might see how easy it'd be for us to get snowed in. A little forbidding, Grace."

She spun the radio dial back and forth as she wiped indigo polish off her nails. The solvent's fumes quickly penetrated the closed room.

"One morning we might wake up and can't get outside. The town hasn't agreed to plow us out. And the Chris-Craft cradled in ice down there in the boathouse . . . well, all I am trying to tell you, Daughter, is that it sure would be nice to have you honor our table. Will you come?"

Grace didn't answer. I stood up and caught her reflection in the bureau's mirror. Even there our eyes didn't meet. I closed her door and walked back downstairs.

"I'm not hungry," I told Alex, who waited dinner in the kitchen. The windows had all frosted up. Outside in the dusk, once again I cleared a path to our car.

Sunday morning we awoke to a howling blizzard. The winds came out of the northeast and blew snow off the lake's surface. By noon the drifts were literally five to eight feet deep about the base of our house. We couldn't see the car, and the road still had not been plowed. Alex and I'd spent most of our time over the past week huddled about the kitchen stove or the console Atlantic in the adjacent living room. One entire block of the house, the summer section, we didn't broach and slept upstairs across from Grace's room. Scarce heat rose up through the floors' registers.

Alex, who'd attempted to keep a bright face through the father-daughter standoff, had begun to noticeably weaken—as I had. Grace hadn't eaten in over nine days. Snow she "drank." We could see the clean window sills. Periodically I'd linger outside her room, listening to the top forty, debating if I should go in and reason with her. But after watching her getting ready to go out Saturday evening, I'd turn away.

We'd even sung "Good morning," through her door each day. Grace never answered. And Sunday, as I pulled my boots on and began layering myself once again with sweaters and a mackinaw to begin to tunnel out of the drifts, I turned to Alex. She gazed out the fixed French doors that served as the kitchen's exterior wall. The lake's surface was blurred by flurries.

"I can't stand this hostile environment we're encountering outside, plus a spiteful daughter waiting us out in that summer's conceit upstairs. One of them I might endure . . . but I'm losing."

Barely a half-dozen years older than Grace, Alex didn't respond. It wasn't how she planned it either. Our arriving at the Lodge in late July, its foundation azaleas blooming in an explosion of colors, the watercraft floating like winged insects out on the lake, the cool interior of the Lodge's summer living room that opened up to floor-to-ceiling screens on three sides shaded by massive hemlocks. Wicker on the veranda. The dream that back on Houston Street we burned like mantle candles. Unable to imagine winter in that half-light, we signed the lease. Yet now it was abundantly clear: summer in Maine was, at best, a beguiling kiss of winter's ten-month frigid embrace. The growing drifts threatening to isolate Alex, Grace and me from the now less-than-quaint general store and town.

My daughter playing "dress up," waiting to go out in her mother's "silk" shoes and stockings. Her hair now brushed to a honey sheen and lying stiff under a mound of pastel wool blankets, listening to the top forty, again, again.

"It's getting to me, Alex."

"She's starving herself, Lee."

No longer convinced she wasn't, I went outside to shovel. The snow was so impacted by the heavy winds that I was able to tunnel, literally tunnel, several feet into it. *I could gopher down the 100 plus feet to the car.* But the thought unsettled me further; I didn't like what it portended. Enough child's play. And began knifing the snow tunnel open with the shovel's blade. Three hours into the project—I had to keep doubling back because of the incessant winds causing more snow to be lifted off the lake's surface and cast against the Lodge and me—I made a decision.

And tramped straight up to Grace's room. Didn't even knock. She sat upright in her bed holding a hand mirror, rubbing the frost away, and painting her cheeks magenta.

"OK," I stammered. "You've won. Tomorrow morning I'll drive you back to New York. I did my damn best. Thought you and I'd get to know each other better up here in the woods. But I can't fight the winds and blizzards, keep the fires going to get us through the winter without perishing—and fight you starving yourself a fairy queen's death. It's gotten to me."

Out beyond the swept window sills, the ledge loomed black and fortress like. Snow had been scrapped there, too.

"You can wear those damn shooting-star stilettos home tomorrow. That please-fuck-me dress, too. And the perfume you bathe yourself in for Ralph—Christ, he sure must be pining for you. Well, goddamnit, so was I—not for my old wife—but for you, Grace. My kid daughter. Whom I've never had the pleasure of knowing. But she's gone, too, huh? Ralph's girl now.

"Just like your Mama. I was never the man of her dreams either."

I cut into the drifts more determined now. Another hour I'd reach the Scout. Then pray the town plow would make its yellow-caution light presence known, flickering down the backside of Lake Christopher. When I heard the kitchen door slam—I suspected Alex had come out to assist.

But it was Grace.

Standing knee-high in fishing boots, a man's winter coat and stiff seersucker trousers she'd found hooked in one of the many Brahmin's closets. Staring at me, shivering, her chestnut hair blowing and catching the lake snow like a gossamer net—her green eyes catching mine like they hadn't in the ice room's bureau's mirror.

"What do you want me to do?" she asked.

"Stay," I cried.

The next morning I walked her out the long camp road. We'd all gotten up early and had hot cereal for breakfast. We could hear the school bus pick up another youth just up the main road. Neither of us had much to say. Grace was dressed in the black rayon dress for her first day of school in Maine, all disguised by my wool mackinaw. In one hand she carried a lunch—in another, a paper bag holding something mysterious. At peace now. But her head was uncovered. We'd even laughed among ourselves over dinner the night before about the capricious pictures of Maine, the house and the pond, we stored in our minds back in the city. And when she looked down through the stand of yellow beech and oak trees to the lake that glistened like a frosted mirror, she said it was unwelcoming—but lovely. I thought it was, too.

At the camp road's end, she motioned that I follow her off to its side where she braced herself against an ancient maple. The school bus would appear any moment.

"Help me, Dad," she said, reaching out her arm to brace it on my shoulder—then stooped to unfasten her galoshes—green uglies she called them. Alex'd bought her a pair at the General Store. She handed me first one, then the other. Black hose, the shade her mother always wore, tottering over the snow.

"Hand me the paper bag, please." Out came the stiletto heels with the shooting-star clasps.

I placed her green uglies in the paper sack.

"Set it alongside the tree, Dad. I'll wear them in tonight."

I watched the bus pull up and its occupants peer out as she climbed aboard, some much younger than she, some who looked older—maybe even as old as Ralph. Grace opened my mackinaw and sauntered down the aisle exactly like I'd expect a New York City woman in wintertime would.

PORTMANTEAU

I've a habit of dragging people around.

Only matter is you couldn't tell. My chalk stripe navy blue worsted suit, white shirt, foulard tie, and the calfskin cap toe shoes disguise my baggage. An hour or two over a drink you still wouldn't know what I really do.

It varies from month to month just how many. There are some regulars. The jazz pianist, the preacher, the worrier, the teary-eyed sentimentalist, the callow youth, and the woman with alba skin and hair the shade of fire. They only show themselves when I'm alone. At such times they exhale collectively and appear.

My wife, Alma, they've taken to, however. Each has slept with her. I don't object whereas you might think I would. I'm not a voyeur. Instead I'm enlightened by the delight she enjoys in the diversity. Each causes her to reveal a different side of herself.

For instance, the keyboardist. He seduces her by whistling chord progressions of one of her favorite ballads. First he'll announce the chords in each bar, say, "OK, C minor seventh, F seventh, D minor, C sharp diminished, then back to C minor and F seventh." Then he'll warble the changes.

All the time rubbing the small of her back, always a prelude to coitus.

The woman with the alba skin and fiery orange hair, she I like to think is a Rabbi's daughter. She's very long legs and fingers that you might imagine are a cellist's. Her lips are a deep vermillion and bud like. When she laughs they open niggardly suggesting a violet breathing behind them. Alma enjoys the reticence of the Rabbi's daughter. How she approaches her with stealth and a fragrant breath. The tongue caresses Alama's neck and aureoles with deliberatenss. Alma giggles and shivers. The Rabbi's daughter moves down the body.

Soon legs are entwined. And Alma is singing the keyboardist's progressions. The Rabbi's daughter's only sound is a sustained A sharp, two octaves above middle C.

The preacher gets her attention only on week nights when Alma returns home from work literally exhausted. He's insistent in his own guarded way. "I don't see enough of you. Don't you love me anymore? Let me massage your feet. Tell me the problems you encountered at the office today." All his tired lines. One invariably works. Especially the massage or his share-your-troubles ploy.

Invariably Alma and he ride off to a perfunctory release. Neither is too excited about it. The preacher for all his earnestness is unable to touch these parts of Alma that the keyboardist and Rabbi's daughter provoke.

When I watch them an ennui sets in. Often I fall asleep before he moves to the missionary position.

The lachrymose sentimentalist places a photograph of Alma's deceased mother over the headboard. Looks very much like Alma actually, when I first met her. The mother is sitting in a wing chair smoking and laughing. Her legs are crossed and a pleated skirt falls just above her knee. The mother's eyes are illumined with a "you're winning me over" smile. There's a very seductive message in the way she has tossed back her head, the long braid flying out to the side of her lovely face with abandon.

A maudlin sadness generates the couple's embrace. Alma's deceased father was a stone, a providential husband and father, but a stone nonetheless. The libidinous nuance suggested in the photograph went unanswered by him. Alma mourns for her mother's loss both while she was alive and now. The sentimentalist sobs and commiserates with her. A prelude to an embrace. A release from this sadness and all the others they can think of.

The callow youth she addresses as the instructor. "Do this. Oh, please, not that. This. Yes, that's better." It's a very small step removed from masturbation. At times she prefers the latter but he'll get better she reassures herself.

Only out of some wizened sense of charity does she prevail the worrier to come in off the balcony (He's always threatening to leap) and accompany her in the bed. She knows that this effort of mercy will be fruitless however; at sometime during the night she will hear the slider doors to the balcony open and see the shadow of the worrier shuddering alongside the wrought iron balustrade and staring ten floors below.

. . .

Alma thinks I'm shallow. She doesn't like the way I cock my hat to one side of my head. Forever she is scolding me that the part in my hair is crooked. "Did you look in the mirror, Edward?"

Little does she know about looking in a mirror. She glances in one and sees her gums receding, the strands of gray, the mole under her left eye which she calls a beauty mark. I see those characters smirking at me. I can't afford to look in a mirror for God's sake.

Alma treats them better than she does me. In fact they are deferential to her. Catering to all her needs. It's me they are indifferent to. "Get a life," they say. And when the worrier ratchets up his anxiety about wanting to leap off the balcony, the others begin to exhibit signs of anxiety. They whisper among themselves, seeking some way to ease him back to stability. "We'll miss him terribly," one will cry. "We're family," another will assert. It's as if one of their members is threatened, they all are. If one bolts on his own volition, underneath all the fuss is a sense he'll pull the others like catfish on a string along with him.

No, they are never solicitous with me. Yet it is I who carry them about on my back. It's why I've come up with this scheme.

I'm going to force the worrier to leap. He keeps threatening obviously gaining some satisfaction from the rest being solicitous of him. Coddling him. I say if he wants to do it, he should be brave and leap. That's the way I will frame the issue. "Worrier, if you keep threatening to leap I believe you are only doing it for the pity the others heap upon you. They don't want to be left alone. Further, I suspect that if you do in fact leap, one will come down with the desire to do the same. It's infectious, you know? This desire to take one's life. I would never consider it. Oh no. But you have. Yet, unlike the others, I have no sympathy for you. Further, I think you are pusillanimous. A coward, yes. I would have much more respect for you if indeed you were brave and took the plunge. It would all be over in a matter of seconds. But a word of advice, stay clear of the tree. It might break your fall. The last thing you need is to finally muster the courage to leap then have the grand event be compromised by your getting hung up in its branches.

"Ignominy. You've suffered enough of that, Worrier.

"So what do you say? I will accompany you early A.M. to the balcony, and in the morning's gray mist, you'll fly. How does that sound? Better than taking the leap. Huh? Is it a date?"

My scheme.

If the worrier does indeed climb upon the balcony's railing, and if the other characters in my charge are convinced of his determination to plunge . . . it's at that very point in time they will flee my head like starlings out a barn loft. For where the worrier goes they follow. His fate will be their fate. And that's when every character looks out for himself. I'm convinced of it.

Alma will have a new man come daybreak.

STAR-CROSSED

My brother used to scrub bodies in a mortuary.

"I like the Packard V-12 hearse Slade Hyde owns. I want to own one someday."

"Doesn't it get to you?" I asked.

"What?"

"The—how should I say it?—detailing the stiffs."

"Only when they got holes in their heads," he answered.

I worked for a florist in Hebron delivering gladioli arrangements to funeral homes, jonquils to mothers of newborns in the hospital, and pink carnation wrist corsages with pipe cleaners to prom dates. Service people had to enter mortuaries through the rear, past the hearse, flower car, and limousines. The shade of Slade Hyde's 1930 Chrysler and Packard fleet was deep purple. Set off from the fleet sat an exquisite hearse with elaborate carved mahogany paneling around and under the oblong windows in its viewing compartment . . . and lying naked on a metal table opposite the driver's side was Hebron's eminent surgeon, Willard Dodge. Tom was scrubbing the doctor's chest with Bon Ami and a horse-bristle brush.

"Tom."

"Jesus Christ, don't ever do that!" he cried, damn near soaking me with the hose.

"What are you doing?"

"Readying him for display."

Everyone in Hebron knew Willard Dodge. He always wore a stiff, white collar fastened with a gold stud, no tie, and a tailored, black worsted suit. The word around town was that he specialized in "women's problems." Tom and I had no idea what that meant, but we thought he must be a good sawbones because we couldn't figure out Ma. Couple of times we heard Father suggest she ought to arrange to see physician Dodge.

"Can't get old Doc's head wet," Tom said.

I was still holding the basket of gladioli with a saffron ribbon stuck in it. Gold script letters pasted on the ribbon read B.P.O.E.

"Slade Hyde's still working on it."

Tom shut off the hose and gestured I look closer. Well, the right side of Willard's head had been packed with a sealing wax the same shade as the rest of his skin. The doc had no eye, no socket even.

"Where's his left eye?"

"Blew it away."

"Christ."

"Half his face, too. But Slade . . . he's like an artist I tell you. Once he puts the marble back in Willard's head, powders some blush back into those jaundice cheeks of his . . . why, under the proper lighting conditions the mourners be whisperin' to old Willard like he were takin' a nap.

"Come here, James, I want to show you something."

Tom opened the doors of a giant metal cabinet, a walk-in closet set against the wall of the cavernous garage. On one side were shelves of car door handles, carburetor heads, boxes of spark plugs, distributor caps, oil filters, wiper blades, waxes and polishes, floor mats; and on the opposite side, trays of eyes—every shade imaginable—false teeth, reading glasses, drawers of toupees, vials of coloring to shade the paraffin wax, limb prostheses, plus a separate compartment where mourning suits and dresses of every vintage hung.

"Why'd the old doc do it, Tom?"

Willard Dodge lived in the finest estate in town alongside the Masonic Cathedral. The shingled house had a magnificent piazza appointed with wicker furniture and chintz pillows; in the summer, ladies gathered there for tea and, later, croquet on an enormous lawn that stayed sylvan green when the rest of the grass in Hebron burnt to straw.

"I heard Slade Hyde gossiping to his driver."

"And . . ."

"Seems Willard was havin' trouble seeing."

"Jesus, that isn't any reason to kill yourself."

"Didn't aim the shotgun down his trousers."

We both glanced at the dead man's member.

"Guess it was the eyesight," I said.

"Uh-huh. But you never know for sure."

It wasn't like Tom to be reflective. Seems washing down the deceased of Hebron was causing him to step back from life. Maybe even pondering his own mortality . . . though he was too damn young.

Tom snapped a white sheet free of its folds and fanned it over the corpse. "That's the one I want," he said, pointing to the purple Packard Phaeton V-12 hearse. "Ain't she a beauty."

If I could remove myself from the vehicle's one and only reason for being, yes, it was one of the loveliest carriages I'd ever encountered.

"What would you ever do with it?" I asked.

"Drive it across America."

"With anybody in it?"

"You, maybe."

. . .

Perhaps it was Doc Willard's choice on the method for leaving town. Tom whistling while he was washing the old man down . . . but thinking about the allure of dying with a splash. Who knows?

In Hebron there existed an unnatural desire to escape the town's sentence. Classmates dreamed of becoming movie stars. World War II's close soured the rhapsodies of young men becoming Audie Murphy. Some of us would rise to the level of Union Trust bankers or J. C. Penney store managers, but most would manually toil the remainder of our lives for Bell Telephone, Neshannock Pottery, or the Johnson Bronze Company. Not much in between.

One classmate, Julie Kramer, had applied to air hostess school. We held a grand sendoff party in her honor. Within six months she reappeared and secured a position with the billing department at Penn Power Company. *The sentence.* Air hostess school, we collectively believed, would free Julie of Hebron's gravitational pull.

Yet nobody in our extended family had ever broken loose.

Father's brother traveled with the Mills Brothers Circus for fifteen years . . . but he returned home. A sign painter today, Uncle lives up alongside Gaston Park in a bungalow where his wife kept vigil for him all those years. "Always believed he'd show up one day on the porch stoop," she said.

Of course, their children were all grown by the time Luke Jakes reappeared, his barrel chest concave and wracked by a catarrh cough.

• • •

I believe Tom studied the dead at Hyde's mortuary instead of his purported lusting for the antique Phaeton Packard hearse. The stiffs were the exclamation points on the uneventful sentences the citizenry of Hebron served. After hosing down so many of them, a man's destiny sinks in pretty fast. "One day somebody will be scrubbing my body down. A piddling wash job, a hair comb, some talc, and a set of mourning clothes . . . their trousers pauper's cloth, cardboard-soled shoes—stage props."

Didn't matter if it was a male or female cadaver—the only real public recognition that it once walked and breathed appeared in the *Hebron Chronicle's* obituary notice.

Mary Hartman, aged fifty-two, the final thirty of those years as a cashier at Murphy's Five and Ten on Washington Street. No surviving kin.

• • •

The day Slade wheeled Willard Dodge, M.D., into the mortuary's garage and unzipped the body bag, I know seeded the notion just how my Tom would deny the town its judgment. The physician had held the shotgun barrel up to his left eye and fired. The other stiffs had merely succumbed, but old Willard took matters firmly in his hands and blew himself off Hebron's stage—in style.

Got a front page headline in the *Chronicle*. Townsfolk began wagging their tongues about the woman-healer's masterstroke. The viewing room in Slade Hyde's mortuary would be standing room only for many afternoons and evenings. Yet not one citizen could recall how Mary Hartman expired.

It's the only reason I offer for what transpired that radiant Sunday afternoon one August.

Several days earlier, Tom showed up at our house mid-day, declaring he'd quit Slade and was joining the Air Force. He wanted to become a pilot.

Well, to me it sounded like one of those faded dreams that fueled us when we'd file out of a movie theater on Saturday night thinking we were Jimmy Dean or Marlon Brando, hop in our cars, and our girlfriends would suspend their disbelief for a night—or maybe a weekend. But we all knew that was a lie. Time to accept the *sentence*, in our case, like men. Tom was having trouble swallowing his.

"A pilot!" I said. "Hell, you're a runt. Plus, you ever see a four-eyed pilot?"

"You'll see," he said with a splintered grin.

A World War II Spitfire airplane sat tethered by guy wires in front of the Hebron's landing strip. Just like a Civil War cannon sat anchored in concrete on its square. Tom was fancying climbing into that fighter aircraft, pulling on a leather helmet and aviator's glasses, flashing a thumbs-up signal from its frosted cockpit—then thundering off into the sky. A man-sized desire of what Julie Kramer had fantasized. All these dreams were the same—one way or other, a Quixote was going to catapult to glory.

"You see yourself in the cockpit of that relic Spitfire at Hebron Landing, don't you?" I asked.

"Matter of a fact, yes."

"It got no engine. War's over. You'll be pushing papers in some damn sweltering office in Georgia or Alabama if you join the Air Force."

Well, come that Sunday, Pap got a call. It was the police.

"Nobody in the car?" Pap asked.

"No, sir."

"Where's my son?"

Wasn't a response.

"I said do you know where Tom—he's my son—d'ya know where he is? He was driving that vehicle."

"Hebron Memorial."

"Well, Jesus have mercy, sir, can you tell me what happened?"

"Don't quite know for sure, Mr. Jakes."

I'd an idea, but was loath to share it with the old man. When we borrowed the neighbor's car to go out to Lawrence Country road and see for ourselves, my only concern was what kind of news did Tom intend to make?

Then I remembered the Spitfire.

Alongside our old Ford Fairlane that Tom had borrowed from our old man that morning lay an empty 5-gallon tin of gasoline. The hood of the car was propped up and its driver's side door hung wide open. The front seat's upholstery was singed and stank of burning hair. Across the road a trail of charred grain stubble ran like a scar through the alfalfa field. The path the width of a man running with his arms flapping.

Wearing the isinglass goggles, a leather bombardier's jacket, its sheep fur collar turned up about his neck, Tom hadn't quite got airborne. First, he was going to fly over the house, buzz our bedroom window, shoot me the bird from the open cockpit—then circle twice before heading off to slam into the Ulysses S. Grant statue in the center of Hebron's diamond. One mighty conflagration.

Screw the measly *Chronicle's* obituary.

Pap hesitated outside Tom's hospital room.

"Let's go in," I urged. "He ain't going to surprise us."

Pap gently pushed open the door.

Kid brother was coiled in cerecloth, the nurse holding a cigarette at his lips. He'd take a drag then in a studied arc she'd lift it off his lips before flicking the ash.

He greeted us with his signature wry grin.

"What were you thinking about, son?"

"Gettin' off the ground."

"Damn difficult, huh?"

She gave him another drag.

"You left a mighty nasty scar in Scroggin's alfalfa, boy. Like a bolt of lighting blazed a trail right through it . . ."

"Fire makes you run, Pap."

Tom laughed, only it sounded tinny, as if it had been transcribed.

"I looked across the field and seen this boy yelling for me to beat my wings harder. He was flapping his arms. Then I saw his mother come out on the porch, and she too began waving her arms in the air. Down field I spy this old farmer in bib overalls. He'd a spade shovel and was twirling it on his hands like a baton. Mouth open wide and out of it rose the whistle of a propeller—*whirring, whirring* . . . for me to get airborne.

"The whole lot of them boosting me on.

"But my wheels, my sticks—I could hear pieces of the aircraft cracking in midair. Cracking like maple kindling. And then I knew—Jesus Christ, I cried, *I'm on fire!*

"D'ya hear, Pap, I'm, on FIRE!"

Father bent over Tom like he was checking under a car's hood. The nurse doused the cigarette in the palm of her hand.

"What can I do for you, boy?" Pap said.

"Hold me," he said.

"You freezing?"

"Did you open a window, ma'am?" Tom cranked at the nurse.

Her arm rose to gesture she hadn't. It's shadow fell like a crow on the window shade.

• • •

To this day I wonder if the boy relished the irony of riding in the Simonized Phaeton V-12, his sweet countenance gazing over the Hebron countryside as the cortege motored to marble hill. Slade Hyde in the driver's seat, attired in a livery coat and chauffeur's hat with the patent-leather bill, me alongside. Father and friends snaking behind. Our headlights illuminating broad daylight. We passed the antique Spitfire, it's shark snout missing a propeller.

The cortege excruciatingly slow.

Are we moving, or is the countryside slowly passing us by? I wondered. Ten automobiles back sat Julie Kramer, *sans* her hostess wings, wearing a navy blue empire dress and white leather belt with matching pumps, excused for the morning to pay respects to somebody else who crashed.

COMBUSTION

Westley McCool's young life centered about the Rose Avenue block on which sat a United Presbyterian Church, a parish house, one ballfield, two dozen nondescript bungalows, and a mortuary. Church, of course, occupied most of Sunday with Bible class, the parson's lugubrious sermon, then evening worship. Saturday and after school until dusk were spent playing ball, except in winter when firemen flooded the park for ice hockey.

Seemed as if most every week there was a church supper in the neighborhood. Long collapsible dining tables were set up in the church basement where the fathers fried kielbasa and eggs—occasionally pancakes on Saturday—and the mothers scrubbed pots and pans.

Upstairs in the vaulted sanctuary, a procession of celebrations paraded through each year: weddings, baptisms, confirmations, calendar events like Easter, Christmas, and even secular holidays. The Fourth of July, Pastor Yates gave a flag-on-a-stick to each congregant as heavy-busted deaconesses in red, white, and blue mufti sashayed with tambourines in the nave to an abridged Tchaikovsky's *Fifth* performed with all its bells and whistles by the organist.

The church was as busy as the ballfield.

Then there was the mortuary on the periphery, virtually an afterthought to the Rose Avenue nexus. Westley's friend Harry Edwards' father owned the place. (Harry always had the finest outfielder's or catcher's mitt, the fullest array of football gear—

shoulder pads, shin and hip guards, Wilson helmets.) The funeral home—Harry lived upstairs—appeared to be joined at the hip to the church, however. The deceased were gurneyed out of the Edwards Home and across the alleyway into the sanctuary for a pastoral "goodbye" prior to their long trek to Castlewood cemetery. Also, mortician Edwards, a deacon of the church, collected Sunday offerings and officiated at lesser occasions—like the Fourth of July service, for instance, while Pastor Yates hovered in the chancel playing Uncle Sam's doppleganger.

Westley and his friends dismissed the symbiosis as another mystery of adulthood they couldn't fully comprehend. Until one summer day an errant softball rolled down the alleyway and into the mortuary's preparation room. The door happened to be ajar. Mrs. Ellwood, the organist, overcome by the sweltering July heat, had passed away in the choir loft several days earlier, and Jack Kelly, who was playing right field, returned with a damp softball and a mordant tale: Grace Ellwood lay on a soapstone slab without a stitch of clothes on, and Harry's father, wearing yellow rubber gloves, was hosing her down just like he did his Buick hearse. The dead always look so seraphic in the coffin, thought Westley. Now how was he going to erase this picture of sweet Grace out of his head?

Girls didn't take part in the ballfield's activities. The Bible and public school teachers forced the two sexes to participate in pageants, spelling bees, and chalkboard eraser cleaning, but as far as Westley and his friends were concerned, the young ladies stuck out there on the border of their nexus like the mortuary—until Red Rollins happened by. The Rose Avenue gang loitered at the far end of the ballfield a September Saturday, awaiting a gathering large enough to pick up sides. They all looked up to Red because he was twenty and played shortstop for the Jackson Flats All-Stars. Smoking Lucky Strikes and razzing the young ones about how none of them could catch a fly ball with a collection basket, Red stood about the open fire Edwards and Kelly had made to take the chill off the morning. When suddenly he pulled out his pecker and began pissing into the embers.

"See how red that son of a bitch is, guys?"

All the boys stared at Red's ardent cock. Westley saw it as luminescent red, like it might have been scalded.

"That's what happens when you fuck Slug."

Slug, who was a couple years older than Westley and his friends, lived on Gaston Road at the squalid edge of the neighborhood.

"She spent last night at my house. My mom went away for the weekend. All of Jackson Flats team showed up. I never met a hotter cunt in my whole life. Too bad she'll either be married or an old whore by the time your puny peckers are ready."

Red folded his back into his trousers.

After he departed, nobody seemed to be interested in picking up sides. Moribund, the boys all agreed to meet later on in the day. Westley tramped down the street to Hanlyn's Market where his mother worked Saturdays driving a Chevy delivery van. The sight of Red's angry member continued to haunt him, but he couldn't quite understand why . . . excepting a smoldering sensation had erupted in the pit of his stomach. He didn't want to play ball either.

Ruth McCool had already gone out on her grocery route. Next door at the shoemaker's, Westley talked with his old friend Sal, when who should walk in but Slug. After a long night of servicing the Jackson Flats ball team, she looked quite normal. Like she'd just washed the dishes and tidied up her mother's house. What was the womanly equivalent to an inflamed pecker, he wondered?

"Westley McCool. How are you this morning?" Slug chirped.

Westley nodded, wondering how she knew his name and embarrassed for what he was thinking—her lying in Red's mother's living room, naked, "giving it" to the third baseman and catcher. He couldn't quite picture it, but it agitated the molten sensation.

Red said she was "hot." And the rubescent penis appeared to be a truth indicator. Slug explained to Sal how she wanted new heels and cleats on her pumps. Westley couldn't help but think she was a grass fire in August standing there at the linoleum counter. Even Sal was getting hot. He flirted with Slug, just as Westley guessed all men did. Naked in the middle of the burning meadow, the heat radiating out of her seductive smile and all the neighborhood men standing at its periphery, entranced. Excepting the womenfolk weren't empathetic.

But when Red told the story of Slug Alexander, it cracked the fragile spine of the orderly Rose Avenue calendar of events, the continuous fun at the ballpark. It shifted the church, mortuary, and ballpark's center of gravity. Episodes of greater interest now took place outside the nexus. Church suppers and the Christian cum patriotic services—Harry Edwards, the mortician's son, kept attending. Westley begged off.

Then one Friday night walking home from a movie, he took the back alley alongside the church and the ballfield when he encountered a cluster of his friends braced against Pastor Yate's double garage doors *ya hooing*.

"Goddamn it, she sure is hot!"

Slug's husky voice erupted."Easy, Red. Take it *easy*!"

"See how long you can keep it in, Rollins," Jack Kelly yelled.

"The bitch is *too* hot," Red cried. "I can't!"

It could have been Pastor Yate's DeSota they were discussing if it were daylight, for the Reverend was always tinkering with its engine, the neighborhood youths bent over the fenders handing him tools.

Instead, they were doing Slug again.

Not the Jackson Flats team. But Red and Westley's ball-playing buddies. Even Harry Edwards. The mortuary was dark with no corpses in attendance that weekend.

"Give me a try at her," Harry begged.

"Too hot for you, boy," Red explained. "Your pecker's got to leather up first. Go do Peggy Hogsham or Becky Flansberg. (These were tenth graders.) You just can't jump in and dick the majors. Can he, Slug?"

Westley heard Slug's derisive laughter. Red whooped and hollered some more, giving a stellar back-alley performance to Westley's teammates. Then he boasted about *"Blowing the eyes out of the eagle!"* Slug and Red momentarily warbled gutturally.

• • •

Westley observed later that evening in bed that his member, when erect, didn't stick out horizontally as he thought it must, but angled up off his torso at 45 degrees. *How could Red push Slug against the garage doors and stick his thing in her?* It doesn't make sense. Westley anxiously wrenched his into a 90 degree angle, but it hurt bad. If my cock sticks off my stomach like a checkmark, how do I go "in and out"? he asked himself.

What intrigued him even more was Red's ranting about how *fiery* Slug's vagina was. Then it began to make perfect sense to him. The inside of Slug's—or any woman's—body was a combustion chamber so volcanic, a man had to move his cock in and out quickly so as not to get scalded. That's why Red's looked like a boiled frankfurter that cold, drizzly Saturday.

"You got to leather them up first for the big time, boys!" Red admonished. "Your balls fall off your baby asses like acorns if you go straight to the top."

• • •

Somebody was lying. His father never broached the subject. Pastor Yates certainly didn't. No evidence of "sex" ever surfaced about his house on Rose Avenue. But then again nobody had the glow that Red or Slug had either—or even the scent. There was a peculiar *fragrance* of sex. The women in Westley's church smelled like Crisco, but Slug, well, she smelled like singed rabbit fur. It was that damn grass fire again, thought Westley. Smoldering in the woods, under all the moss and the leaves. A fire underfoot. The earth is stove hot. Slug is stove hot. And he couldn't take his mind off either of them. Mr. Edwards hosed down the organist. Was he making certain her grass fire was out? Incandescent in the coffin when they shut the lid? Distracting Westley. He'd drop fly balls in left field. Flub questions in class. All because of Slug.

As cold weather returned, the boys only wanted to sit around discussing the 'in and out,' and keep on the lookout for Red, hoping he'd stop by to regale them with more exploits. They sniffed around Slug, too, whenever she was out on the street. A few tried to follow Red's consul about leathering up, but Hogsham and Flansberg weren't cooperating. The firemen didn't flood the ballpark that winter either. Even in December, the unquenched simmering that'd erupted inside Westley that Saturday morning with Red's tale, hadn't abated one bit.

Until one February Saturday afternoon, Westley was returning home from work at the florist shop, when two classmates called out to him as he crossed the street. Other than to say hello in the school's corridors, he didn't know either of them. They lived on the south side of town, and one of them, Estelle Santangelo, said she had something to tell him. The girls stood under the Wetzel's Gun & Pawn Shop three-brass-ball sign.

"Marie here has a crush on you, Westley."

Marie Wyoming, standing alongside Estelle, was an attractive brunette, slightly overweight, who chewed gum.

"Yeah?" Westley answered.

"Tell him what you want to do, Marie."

Marie turned to watch her reflection in the gun shop window and began snickering.

Westley turned red.

"She wants to take it all off for you, Westley, and show you her blushing tits . . . this very afternoon in her mother's bedroom. Nobody's home. Whadoya say?"

The big time, thought Westley. Christ, here it is. I ain't even prepared.

"Oh, I got to go home to supper."

"Say you had to work late, Westley. Come on home with us. Have fun."

The setting sun caused the buildings' shadows to angle out over the street in coal-black patches. Westley heard the quitting siren sound a mile away at the pottery where his father worked. The trio began walking toward the viaduct. Estelle walked on ahead, singing. Marie hung back, occasionally brushing up against him, ratcheting up his blood heat. Soon the pair were walking hand in hand. Estelle laughed and began skipping farther ahead until she was out of sight. On Electric Street, they spotted her sitting on Marie's porch swing waving them on.

"Nobody's home, Marie. Hurry."

Westley followed the girls onto the porch and into the shuttered house. The steps to the second floor were opposite the front door. Marie took Westley's hand and led him up into the narrow hallway into her mother's bedroom. Lace curtains breathed in and out the open window and oval framed portraits of a much earlier wedding couple hung askew on either side of the bureau's mirror. Estelle sat down on a straight back chair. Marie sat Westley at the foot of the bed and pulled the pale green chenille spread off the pillows. She lifted a box of nose powder off a chiffonier and, with a flesh-colored puff, slapped it onto the mattress. Puffs of apricot-scented talc exploded off the sheets. Westley watched as she pulled down the green opaque shade then undressed, standing before him in her bra and panties—glowing.

Westley thought about many things, all of them about the grass fire that now blazed out of control at the pit of his torso and haloed Marie—and how his checkmark pecker stood at military attention. Shit, he didn't know the first thing about *screwing*. Furthermore, he wasn't about to stand Marie up against the water-stained floral wallpaper with Estelle sitting there looking on. Until she stood and, with Marie's assistance, tenderly opened his trousers, all the time looking straight into his eyes and smiling. Marie lay on the bed with her undergarments off and her legs open. She slapped the powder puff on her triangle, turning the beard a feverish coral.

God, thought Westley, why is this all moving so fast? The fire nimbusing her white flesh, the cloying scent of fruit, and yet he had to somehow walk through those flames, and lie on top her Jell-O body? Estelle had now lifted his trousers and dropped his shorts below his knees. She stood away and smiled at her friend, then returned to the chair, drawing her knees up to her chest, waiting.

One on the chair, the other on the bed, and Westley standing at its foot, the checkmark pulsating like a neon light clicking on and off at a 24-hour diner. And no sound of fire trucks.

Marie got on her knees and drew Westley into the bed with her.

"Stick it to me," she whispered.

He couldn't move.

"Come on. Pussy got no teeth."

She grasped his cock and, watching the expression on his face ice up, slowly inserted it into her body. Westley squinched his face for the scalding, the dunking of his member into her fuming caldron. Determined that he wouldn't cry out. No matter how fiery she was inside.

Estelle now hunched down on the bed beside the pair, animatedly witnessing Marie initiate Westley McCool into south side's big league. "I'll bet he ain't even leathered up, Marie!" she gushed.

"Westley. Move. *God dammit move,*" Marie wriggled, jerking him smartly upward.

But Westley McCool froze.

Both girls glared at him.

"What's wrong, ain't it no fucking fun?" cried Marie.

Westley was speechless.

"Suck her tits, you prick!" scolded Estelle, giving him a biting slap on his bare ass.

But Westley wasn't moving. Neither in nor out. Marie, in exasperation, shoved him off. Both girls bounded out of the bed and stood over him, boiling. He had a death grip on his pecker.

"What the hell's wrong with you, McCool!" Estelle hissed.

"There weren't no fire," he sighed, watching sadly as a spit of gizum arced meekly out of his cock to trickle onto the chenille spread—boneash.

He was white as a corpse.

LAMENT

Edgar Giles grieved over the loss of his father, his brother, and dog—the last to expire, under the dining room table overnight. When it came time for the morning walk, Fred didn't stir. At the burial service in his backyard that afternoon, Edgar keened so loudly that his neighbor peered over the stockade fence.

"Fred's dead," he sobbed.

"My condolences," the abutter said.

"I don't like how this show is closing."

"Could you explain?" asked the neighbor.

"We keep getting lighter." Edgar flapped his arms in the air to demonstrate. "Parts of us keep falling away. When we were children our fortunes grew. Babies came, along with sofas and automobiles, nieces and nephews.

"Now it's the long goodbye." He glanced at Fred's grave. "He shadowed me during the day. He lay asleep in the sun puddles throughout my house. He answered the door. Barked when the phone rang. Ate the food I found disgusting—licked my face . . ."

Edgar sobbed some more.

He dropped to his knees, scooped a handful of soil from the newly covered grave, and brought it to his face.

"Father, brother . . . now Fred," he mumbled. "Once it was the sky."

That evening Edgar crawled under the table. "I'll sleep here only this evening," he thought. "In remembrance of him."

At some point during the night, he crawled out to Fred's water bowl. "How silly is this?" Yet, it was more comforting than lying upstairs in his double bed, mourning the dog's departure. "Perhaps this is the way we keep our loved ones alive. We embrace our memories of them. Affect their personas."

He curled up close to the back door and heard rustling in the rear yard. A hedgehog, he guessed—and reflexively barked.

"Oh, Christ . . . how absurd!"

But it didn't seem all that bizarre. After all, hadn't he often played woman to his estranged wife, Beatrice, when they made love?

"Loosen my tie, unbutton this stiff white shirt, Edgar, oh yes, unzip my fly," she'd whisper.

Neither of them thought their exchanging roles was depraved. Why, he'd even ask her to lick his non-existent breasts.

Edgar wandered into the living room and stretched out in a puddle of moonlight.

How he missed Beatrice, too. No letters or phone calls. Her clothes, the summer dresses with the robust chrysanthemums she left hanging alongside his suits in the closet. Her open-toed shoes. The pillbox hats with veils. Alongside his shaving cream her cerulean vials of cologne and perfume sat in the medicine chest. He would sprinkle some on her side of the bed after dark . . . then dream she'd slipped into the boudoir to caress him.

A car stopped in front of the house. Edgar ran to the window, yapping. It felt perfectly normal.

At daybreak he was awakened by the newspaper landing on the front stoop. Just as Fred faithfully did each morning, Edgar butted the door open with his nose, clenched the paper in his teeth, carried it to the sunroom, dropped it at the base of his favorite chair—then stood, turned on the coffee pot, and read the day's news.

Later that morning he placed a slice of sod over Fred's grave and decided against memorializing it with a marker. "What's the sense?" he reasoned. "Bone and flesh under that sod, the animal is alive within me. Why couldn't I have understood that sooner?

"None of my loved ones have departed. They are alive inside of me. I simply must be more caring, calling on them more than I ever have. Why, even Beatrice, she will be inside there, too. Father, Brother Jed, Fred, and Beatrice. How fortunate am I? How blessed?"

Following lunch, he undressed, put on Beatrice's ankle-length saffron empire dress flowered with Japanese lanterns and a pair of her coral mules, spritzed cologne under his arms, and returned downstairs to prepare tea.

"Today we'll have my brother over. He and Beatrice always got along."

From the cupboard he chose a package of fancy tea cookies and placed several on a tole tray alongside the fragile porcelain tea cups. In the living room he set them on the glass table with the ornate Oriental walnut base. A Matisse odalisque hung on the side wall. "How charming," he thought, and settled into the plush sofa, awaiting Jed.

But Jed was late.

Soon he thought he heard steps on the front walk. He ran to the door and barked.

"My imagination," he said, and returned to the sofa.

Jed sat opposite him wearing Tasmanian worsted trousers, tassel loafers, and a Bengal striped linen shirt with open collar.

"I've been expecting you, dear Jed," Edgar enthused. "It's been too long. I feared you'd never arrive."

Jed eyed Beatrice closely. Her narrow feet, their high instep, the scent of jasmine. Heady in the shadowy room.

"How lovely you look this spring morning," he said.

Beatrice flushed.

"How's your faithful dog?"

"Immortally sweet and faithful," replied Beatrice.

Jed continued to focus on Beatrice's bodice, to the point that it was making her uncomfortable.

"You know I always wished I'd met you first, before my brother did. You could sense that couldn't you ... all those nights the three of us were together? I secretly lusted after you. How could you fail to divine that, Beatrice?"

"Oh, Jed. We mustn't hurt Edgar. It's unfair."

"Everything is fair when lust is concerned. Tomorrow I could be under the sod. Wouldn't you rather travel to eternity knowing at least two brothers desired you instead of one?"

Beatrice nodded.

There was a sudden knock at the door.

Fred barked.

"Go see who it is," Jed said. "I promise I won't leave."

It was the mailman. A package marked *unable to deliver* Edgar had sent to Beatrice.

Her earrings and some other jewelry she'd left in an etched glass bowl in the corner cupboard. Among the pieces was a gold watch that had stopped ticking decades earlier. It had belonged to her mother, Alba. Edgar knew she wanted the keepsake.

But here it all came back. Address unknown.

The mailman had a milk bone for Fred. "Where's Fred this morning? I thought I heard him."

"Sleeping under the table," Edgar replied offhandedly.

When he returned to the glass table, Jed had disappeared. Edgar's heart sank. He suddenly realized the mailman had seen him wearing Beatrice's dress.

"Oh Jesus Christ!"

Would the neighbors now begin to gossip? He'd have to be more vigilant. Nobody's business who lived in the house. "Surely the mailman has seen more than he cares to admit. Perhaps he didn't even notice. The Freemonts across the street—now who knows what's going on behind their door?"

Edgar finished the tea, but felt saddened.

Why had Jed said what he did? Didn't he know how it would affect him? And why hadn't Edgar guessed it earlier? "I never lusted after his woman," he fumed. "Goddam it, Jed! How could you betray your brother that way?"

He cried out with such rage that Fred started barking and jumping at the window. The sheers keep getting snagged in his paws.

Soon Fred found a shaft of sunlight on the Hariz carpet and began licking himself. The Japanese lantern dress looked winsome on him.

• • •

As the days and weeks passed, the neighbors were surprised to see Edgar Giles walking alone the route he normally strolled with Fred in the morning.

"Something happened to your dog?" one inquired.

"Years have taken their toll on dear Fred. He gets his exercise in the house now, up and down the stairs, in and out of the many rooms." Edgar laughed gleefully. "Yet, this old dog needs to keep moving."

"Of course!" came the cheerful rejoinder.

Edgar appeared such a happy fellow of late. He had a bounce in his step. Not as lugubrious as the neighbors had formerly observed him. He waved to them now. Said *good morning* more frequently. Didn't appear as pensive as he once had.

"You don't suppose he has a new woman, do you?" one neighbor asked another.

"I've seen no evidence of one."

"Perhaps he is just beginning to realize how much better off he is in Beatrice Giles' absence. God, what a harpy was she."

"I always felt sorry for the poor man."

"Well, some serendipity has occurred in his life. God willing we be as lucky."

It was now a full life indeed.

Jed had finally consummated his lust for Beatrice. Fred was eating chicken and steak tips instead of kibble soaked in a tepid broth of tap water. And most satisfying to Edgar were the daily conversations with his father.

Long afternoon conversations like they once enjoyed.

He didn't really mind the Beatrice-Jed mating. Better Jed put up with her than he. Much simpler that way.

There was only one major drawback to this carnival of events for which Edgar was the designated ringmaster.

Nothing saddened him any longer. His loved ones were at his side daily and often late into the evening. Doing myriad duties. He needed nobody. Nothing outside the house. He no longer used the telephone. The mail piled up in the vestibule. Fred continued to bark at outside noises, but Edgar would merely stand a distance away from the windows, staring out the sheers to ascertain who wanted to bother him.

"Please," he muttered. "Just leave us alone."

Then one day as dawn was breaking, he went into the backyard and knelt at Fred's grave. Barely discernable now. With a pocketknife he sliced the sod open and reached into the shallow grave for the box in which he'd swaddled Fred.

Maggots, hundreds of them, scurried out of the cotton cere and up Edgar's arms. He shuddered, lifting what remained of Fred. It was lighter now and felt like collapsing bones, no longer the firm body of the dog that once resided under the dining room table.

Edgar placed the bones back into the container, kicking dirt back over its lid.

He returned to the house and went upstairs into his closet. He lifted out that same saffron silk dress with Japanese lanterns that Beatrice had worn that day to greet Jed, held it close to his body . . . and felt bones. Like dense crickets they gave off clicking sounds when he squeezed. He let the garment fall to the floor.

He scurried into the basement where years earlier he'd helped his father undress in preparation to bathe in the cellar's shower. It's where his father wept before the water flowed out of the bronze rose, washing them of the time they'd wasted calling each other from distant doorways.

And he recalled when he embraced his naked father . . . how he'd felt bones.

They clicked like jacks tossed across a hardwood floor.

Returning to his living room, Edgar called out to Jed, who appeared in the fiery gladiola in the vase on the Chinese table. He could see his image in the watery glass top. Jed was crying for having betrayed him, for having taken Beatrice in his arms and brought her breasts to his fiery mouth.

"They were dry," he told Edgar, "dry and bitter as quince. And when I lay on top of her . . . I heard her bones tapping against each other like a snare drum's funeral march.

"Like the *second line*, Edgar.

"Beatrice is ahead of the second line.

"Hear the snare drum's *tap, tap, tap, tap*?

"Come follow us, brother.

"Beatrice is waving a lime green parasol and marching shoeless over the red clay. Our father is behind her, blind, but closely following Beatrice's japonica scent.

"Then me, dear brother. I'm behind him wearing my pinstriped suit with an orange flame billowing out of my suit jacket pocket, my bare feet kicking up the dust to the tune of clicking bones and the *tap, tap, tap*, of the snare drum.

"Fred at my heels. Snapping at them, the ornery critter.

"Now you, bringing up the line."

Tap, tap, tap.

Edgar never answered the door.

SHE'S A LITTLE STORE INSIDE

My father, Jacob Müller, had three siblings. Alexander the Monsignor, Felix who doubled as a clown and lion trainer for the Mills Brothers Circus—and sister, Eva, who sold her body until it shook too much.

When it came time in Jacob's life to sum it all up, to prepare himself for what might or might not occur after death, he didn't knock on the sacristy door. Instead he sought out Eva and Felix who lived in run-down bungalows on the outskirts of our town.

As a boy I couldn't understand why.

I loved frequenting Uncle Alexander's cathedral with its flying buttresses, its west and east stone towers, one carrying the great bell, the other housing more than one thousand pipes for the electro-pneumatic organ in the baptistry. Monsignor ascended the grand circular staircase in his polychromatic chasuble at High Mass while racks of ruby-red, ink-blue, and clear votive jars bearing flame and melted wax illuminated wooden saints, and morning sunlight filtered through stained glass clerestory windows. And there on the rood screen separating the choir from the nave, a crucifix larger than the statue of Franklin Delano Roosevelt on our village green—Christ's gold-leafed body, mirroring the votive flames. Alive.

Parishioners rising and crossing themselves, kneeling, rising again . . . their solemn incantation echoing Uncle's Latin liturgy.

And Christ on fire.

Why a whore and a clown? I wondered, when Monsignor Alexander owned a golden ring with a giant ruby that his congregants kissed.

"I'm off to the whiskey bar," Father said. I'd clandestinely follow to see if the Monsignor would embrace him in an alleyway minus his surplice, and the two of them would stroll into the backdoor of the parish house.

Instead I watched Father walk wide of the large shadows that the basilica towers, Temperance and Perseverance, cast across Main Street like an ominous embrace.

Aunt Eva sat in the shadows of her porch of summer afternoons. A kewpie doll with rouged cheeks, and hair dyed henna that haloed a china face. Her dress dropped inches above her bony knees. She wore spiked heels painted with fuchsia nail polish and dreamily stared onto the dirt street, her slight body jerking as if a motor oscillated under its bottom. Waiting. Waiting for a blanket of darkness to eclipse the bungalow.

I asked Father what Aunt Eva was selling, since so many men stopped by after dusk.

"She's a little store inside," he said.

Once as I was passing her house she signaled me over.

"I'm your Aunt Eva," she said "You look exactly like Jacob."

"Pleased to meet you," I said.

"Your father chooses to ignore I'm his sister."

I nodded as if I understood.

"You must come by and visit me sometime. We'll get to know each other better." She grinned.

In time I learned what she'd been selling inside her bungalow.

That she took off her bedizened doll clothes for strange men.

Then I dreamed of paying her a call.

I envisioned her standing disrobed in her bedroom, arms outstretched to the door jambs, one foot touching the other, and the henna triangle burning like the bush in the Bible. A smoke of yearning curling out of Uncle Alexander's incense censer.

Her image provoking the ache I brooked for the gold-leafed crucifix.

But as Aunt Eva's tremors grew more conspicuous over time and the traffic upon her walkway diminished . . . so did my ardor and contrition.

Her house was no longer freshly painted a periwinkle blue. Its front steps fell into disrepair. Like a plaster of Paris palmist inside a cloudy glass arcade box she sat staring out her window. You place a nickel into a slot, her wooden hand overturns a Queen of Spades, a cardboard fortune drops out a cupped opening—somewhere, you imagine, below her skirts.

Except a house fly had died on its forehead. Chipped flesh-tinted plaster exposed chalky stigmata. These women in arcade boxes are saints, too, I thought. Lesser saints than those mutely lining St. Margaret's side aisles. Or Christ pinioned against the rood screen— He was the master saint, the biggest and best of all the arcade ones, and those who lived on dirt streets like Aunt Eva, waiting, waiting, for acolytes with jingle in their trousers.

· · ·

Uncle Felix lived one street over from Eva's place. He kept a palomino in a shed behind his modest one-story house. On Independence Day he dressed like Tom Mix and headed a parade down Main Street with paper American flags attached to his steed's halter. He'd painted stars on its hooves and braided its flaxen tail in red and blue ribbon. A large barrel-chested man with chiseled features, Uncle Felix favored an American Indian.

"He could whup lions!" a bystander exclaimed. "Make 'em lie down docile before him like house tabbies."

Felix Müller dramatically swept his Stetson against the sweaty flanks of his golden horse.

"I seen him standin' on the back of a galloping Arabian once," said another, "a pair a six shooters blasting crockery out of the sky that clowns spiraled aloft like barn swallows."

"Was he a trapeze artist, too?"

"If one of those spangled dames dangled by her gams—you bet! He didn't join the circus to get away from 'em."

As the parishioners glowed, minding Monsignor Alexander's vestments sweep the basilica's cobbled floor, the Eucharist chalice ascending to the giant rood, so, too, the town's women in Uncle Felix's wake. Always he'd spot a comely bystander, dismount, and like the gentleman I think he never was, boost her onto the horse's backside. The pair would clop up the pavers past Hutton's hardware, the Episcopal Church, and Post Office, halting before the viewing stand where Uncle Alexander officiated alongside the Mayor and Chief of Police.

Felix's woman gripping his midriff, the horse perspiring under her thighs.

The two brothers locked into each others gaze.

A splinter of wistfulness marred the cleric's severe demeanor. *The bouquet of incense is impotent to satisfy a man's need to scent a woman,* he sighed. *Felix feels the drumming of her heart, her hot breath against his neck.* And for a single blasphemous second he envisioned her splayed against the basilica's apse, a thousand votive candle flames rising up to illuminate her. Alexander blinked, removed his steel rimed frames, and rubbed his eyes, praying the image that returned would be the worthy one.

But she mouthed his name, beckoning he veil her nakedness with his peacock robes.

His malicious brother, Felix, taunting him about women when really all he ever yearned for was salvation.

Felix flashed a sardonic grin, gesturing to the weighty crucifix that hung about his brother's neck.

"He suffered a big letdown, too, Alex."

• • •

Eva sat still as a reliquary on the opposite end of town.

At night when I'd pass her darkened house, I'd fancy her lying in her doll costume upon the bed, it trembling with her.

I wanted to place racks of the illuminated votive candles, the ones in the ruby vases, hundreds along her porch banisters.

In memory, Aunt Eva, of your early self.

How you gave of yourself God knows not for pleasure. Yours certainly.

The laborers, policemen, politicians, even a few wayward clergy, perhaps they could visit you now on St. Eva's Day, and in a palanquin, parade you through our streets while the wives and children of your patrons pin dollar bills to your sanctum sanctorum dress— a zipper down its backside that sang myriad times each day as you stood before us naked as the Word.

What a religious burg it would then be.

The Whore, the Monsignor, and the Horseman who carried six shooters in leather holsters that hung to his sides like enshrined penes.

• • •

But there were no beginnings anymore.

Winter had breathed heavily into Father's ear.

I felt a dark river had coursed its way through our psyche, and I went to him in deep sadness to say that I loved him . . . *and was he afraid as I?*

The gold-plated crucifix I was convinced shivered like Aunt Eva on winter nights when the custodian turned off the gas boilers. That the Neshannock River ran through our town bearing ice.

"Good bye, dear Father," I whispered in his ear . . .

"Don't be rash, Son. It's people's dreams we read on billboards and hear from the pulpits, be those of your sad Uncle's or the halls of commerce.

"I've watched you of late tease the railings of our bridges. *Over a woman perhaps?*

"Look at your Aunt Eva.

"What man would destroy himself over her? Men made of her body more than it could ever be. It's why she took money for it.

"We are simple beings who must create for ourselves grand dreams to compensate for what we don't own.

"Your Uncle Alex flagellates himself for being unworthy of partaking in the body of Christ.

"Felix sticks his head into the mouth of a Lion.

"Aunt Eva screws Mayor Delasandro.

"Who would find pleasure in your careening off the Jefferson Street Bridge?"

• • •

That evening I trailed him through the alleyways to Eva's shadowy house. The door opened before he stepped onto the porch stair as if she'd been expecting him.

After several minutes a flickering ruby votive lamp was placed in the window. *Did he know I was watching for a sign? Had he told her about my dialogue with the river, the dark Neshannock?*

I watched him and Uncle Felix meet on a street corner of a Sunday afternoon. Speaking solemnly to each other as visitors to a wake, the brothers soon embraced and stood motionless for several minutes, studying their shoes before turning their backs to each other.

These were goodbyes.

Then late one balmy night, I heard the sash in the hallway rattling. It alarmed me for I could hear no wind outside. I had my window open, hoping for a breeze to come off the open field behind our house, perhaps a cold draft to rise to off its narrow creek, the runoff from the limestone quarry up our road.

I opened my door.

Father stood in the hallway dressed in a white shirt, black tie—and dancing shoes, the black and white brogues, with no stockings.

His face squashed against the glass.

The vibrations of his deep voice, an incantation of sort, causing the window pane to buzz. But it sounded as if he'd begun crying.

"Kyrie elision.

"Kyrie elision.

"Christe elision."

Fragments of the Mass.

"Father. What is it? What in God's name are you doing?"

"Agnus Dei, qui tollis peccata mundi: miserere nobis."

"Praying for Felix, Eva, and Alexander. For you, for me, for all our sins."

"But why?" I cried.

"Uncle Alexander's censer breathes the foul odor of death. The lights in faces of the saints have been snuffed out—and I can't get my breath."

He turned to me, his eyes as grey as the rood's in the chancel.

"Son, it's all dark out there."

He extended his fingers to stroke my face . . . but faltered.

"Who have these caressed? The scent of those who opened to me . . . their sweet breath gone. *My hands have lost their mind.*

"The bell in the tower cries night.

"Oh Christ!" he cried.

"Give me the crucifix. Give me a clown. Give me a match."

---

* "Lamb of God who takes away the sins of the world have mercy on us."

THE BANDONEON

It was Astor Piazzolla's distinctive tango melody, its lag rhythm, that caused me to wander into the dark passageway that snaked between the city's tall buildings. The tavern door, the only fenestration on a massive wall of brick that fortressed the alleyway, was marked by a crudely sketched killer whale painted Chinese red.

This was a Pennsylvania mill town where accordions customarily played Polish melodies for weddings in large function halls. It had no street musicians, let alone one versed in the Argentinian's book. Dressed in black and wearing a black fedora with its brim snapped over his eyes, he handled the instrument as if he were opening and closing a woman. At intervals the music swelled then whispered—or merely exhaled.

At times one foot dangles over the side of the bed. An arm extends to draw him in, her body unfolding to his touch, opening to the white-sheeted bed as he spreads her arms, the melodic sigh— then he closes her inward once again. The repeat, the repeat.

She's far away as he is, I thought.

The narrow alleyway resonated with the bandoneon's lament.

He lay the instrument on the brick pavement, lighting a cigarette. I stood several yards away in the shadows.

"How is she?" he asked.

"You," he said, staring at the ground. "How is she?"

He had mistaken me for somebody else.

"That widow's dress she wore before anybody had died, does it still fall to her ankles?"

I turned to move back onto Franklin Street.

"Her spiraling jet hair. You never saw it dropping to the top of her white pear-shaped ass did you?" His laughter echoed up the corridor.

"All the good things in life she kept shrouded in mufti and stiff muslin. Her wooden heels ringing through the hallways and empty rooms . . . like the house clock.

"But this instrument, she makes sunlight in this narrow dark space, no? Oh, Christ how I played her . . . the black dress puddling the bedroom floor. The string shoes that clocked her escape to paradise . . . kicked under the bed. The only sound now her murmuring softly to me."

But then, for days after, the garments tied tighter to her bodice. Her breasts cinched tight to her rib cage. Her hair balled up like kite twine and pinned to her skull. Her lips pursed.

"The bandoneon who denied it ever sang.

"*'Don't touch me,'* she'd cry."

Now I knew.

"But she's gone," I said.

"Gone?" he laughed. "*Gone?* We are never gone."

"Who are you?" I asked.

I wasn't certain. The hat's brim . . .

"A musician," he said.

"But how do you know me? Know her?"

I stepped alongside him, hoping to look into his eyes. He recoiled.

"Please, don't!" he said, alarmed. "You mustn't touch me."

He lifted the bandoneon and disappeared into the pub. When I followed, the place was empty save for the bartender who denied anybody had just entered.

"Didn't you hear the accordion outside the door?"

"A wedding party?" he asked.

• • •

Less than a week later I arrived home from work after dark and swore I heard the sound of heels clicking on the floor in the upstairs hallway.

They beat with the regularity of a metronome.

I walked to the base of the stairway. "Hello?"

"So tell me, can you see his bones? How shabby does he *really* look now that he ain't got anybody to look after him—to launder his soiled clothes stinking of booze, piss, and women?"

Like he'd said—she stood at the top of the stairs in widow's weeds and string leather heels. Hair pulled tightly to her head, though now mostly gray, and in a knot fastened with silver pins. About her neck, a lace doily like an antimacassar.

Years earlier when she passed, I sighed with relief. So desperately she wanted to marry Christ. To seek redemption.

By saying, "Don't touch me."

The *click click click* of her shoes. As if in some paradoxical way it was a mockery of his tango beat. No opening or closing . . . only that steady inexorable drip of time.

His time was one of seduction.

Hers, its warden.

"So, do you still shoulder him up the stairs, undress him for bed while he curses you for not being able to enjoy life as he does—then cover his gamy body?

"Does he still rant about how I wasn't the woman he'd have liked me to be? Oh, he loved the *whores*. But *whores* don't raise men like you, huh, Son? Thank your lucky stars that you didn't fall out of a trafficked womb.

"Oh, he slayed the ladies, alright. He killed me to all life's pleasures."

I walked up several steps.

"But he's gone," I said.

"Gone?" A sardonic grin barely cracking her stony expression. "Gone, you say? *Where in Christ's name do we go?*" she cried.

Her hands trembled as if they ached to caress me. When I was a young man she'd gently draw my face close to hers to see what I might be hiding.

I reached out to lure her to me.

"Don't touch me," she murmured. *"You mustn't touch me."*

Then, as quickly as he did, the clicking of her heels ceased. The clock died.

That night as I lay awake the Argentinean strain rose from a floor below while outside my bedroom I heard her beating time . . . but to the melody of penance, the song of dread and waiting.

As if *affirmation* and *denial* had taken up residence . . . once again.

I had known these two people. Each had aptly described their memories of the other. And both were gone within a span of two years. She first.

But why had they returned?

After days and nights of listening to their discord, their canceling out of each other—

"Why?" I asked.

"Why have you come here? Why return to my house?"

He smoked and played his bandoneon. It moved across his knee sensuously. But implicit in each tune he played—no matter how tempestuous, how fiery—was a dark sadness. A spade full of loam always falls back to earth.

Don't permit the beat of your heart to mock you for willing to escape its regularity. The secret is to pretend it doesn't exist and in that dream, rise above it in denial.

"But where did you learn that?" I asked. "You who had a tin ear. You who sang off key, causing your women to break out in laughter. This is a master's music you push and pull."

"We create our own paradise," he answered.

"Mine was here. I only recall it in dreams."

Then I asked her. "But why?" I said.

She leaned against the wall in the upstairs hallway. Her habitual spot as I recall. Outside their bedroom door.

"Why did you return?"

She had stopped pacing.

When I approached, she gestured that I move no closer.

"Please," I begged. "Tell me."

"We're lost," she said. The words barely audible.

"But even worse . . ." she hesitated.

"What is it?" I asked, straining to hear her, moving closer.

Again she shooed me back.

"The irony," she sighed, then yielded a slight grin.

"Ask him to come to the base of the stairs for me, please."

"You want to see him?" I was astonished.

"Yes," she whispered.

She leaned over the bannister, crying out to the room below.

"Will you come up the stairs?"

The bandoneon quit.

"It's getting late you know? I'm not hearing the stairs sigh under your weight. Are you coming?"

The house was as quiet as death.

"Have you fallen asleep down there, Thomas Murphy? You ain't expecting me to wait forever, are you?"

I watched her sink back against the wall.

"What suit's he wearing tonight? Has the crease gone out of its knees? Are its buttons missing? Has he got his big red hand on the bannister? Is he pullin' himself up the stairway?

"Can you smell the liquor on him?

"Will you answer your mother, boy? CAN YOU SMELL THE BOOZE ON HIS BREATH? IS IT FILLIN' THE HOUSE LIKE THE BREATH OF THE DEVIL?

"FOR CHRISSAKE, WILL YOU BE TELLIN' HIM TO HURRY?"

"Why, Mother?" I asked.

"I ain't been touched in paradise," she said.

• • •

The Argentinean would never advance up the stairway—his ban-doneon lying on the kitchen floor. There would come no earthly sounds out of the closed bedroom that night or any other. It was only the yearning that I heard.

"Can't you hear me, Tom?

"Will you touch me?" her refrain.

And his, *"Didn't I tell you?"*

At which point he'd resume squeezing the pleated bellows, turning its louvers alive across his knee. His dreaming aloud.

"I don't hear the wooden steps sighing," she'd scold.

"Where's your black mufti?" he'd retort. "And those coal-dust hose that reached to the very tops of your chalky thighs. Will you be obliging Thomas Murphy help you slide them off the prettiest legs in all of paradise?"

"Can we be touching each other for real?" she cried. But it was a laughing cry.

They'd be no stroking in this Eden either.

I descended the stairs to see him one last time.

"Is that you, Tom? Do I be hearing you climb the steps?"

He stood at the doorway.

"An Argentinean?" I asked.

"Your father," he answered.

"Son . . . tell her I sing for the few simple delights she did give me. The nights she opened and closed to me like a virgin.

"For teaching me how to play like an Argentinean.

"I miss hearing her breathing alongside me. Her keeping time in the hallway.

"Tell her I lusted so for life because she was so damn terrified of it.

"Now neither of us can be touched—the dark irony of it all. She went off to marry Christ. He doesn't even sweat."

I wanted to draw his breath up my nostrils. The drum—I wanted to hear his drum.

But it was the night air that I embraced. The bitter wind off the ocean. I could hear the stones rolling back and forth with every new wave beating the shore. Thousands of rolling balls.

"Will I see you again?" I called into the night.

"Put her to sleep," his words came floating back.

"Let her hear your heavy tread on the stairs. She'll fall asleep in the promise that by morning I'll return home.

"Show me the way to the next whiskey bar. Oh, don't ask why. Oh, don't ask why."

CIRCUS MAN

I try to make sense of it all.

I try to put my house in order.

I try to make amends to those I've transgressed.

Some are no longer here to listen. That hurts.

And those who are . . . my words offer scarce comfort. Perhaps it's better not to say anything at all.

These are the words I found written on a piece of paper folded inside Mother's Bible, which she read each night before turning in. Father always waited until she had turned out the light before undressing and crawling in alongside.

My brother and I were made after the Bible reading.

Father placed his cigarettes on its black leatherette cover over the gilded picture of Christ holding a lantern before a door.

"He stands outside our bedroom door, listening," Sammy said. When the lights in the house were extinguished and everybody was in bed, Sammy'd crawl out of ours and place his ear to the door.

"What are you listening for?" I asked

"The circus man."

"The circus man?"

"Yeah. They pounded nails into his hands and feet, didn't they? He's some courageous dude. I want to hear his breathing."

There were nights we heard nothing.

Then we did.

"Come here, Tom," he whispered. "Listen. Hurry!"

I slipped out of bed and put my head alongside his against our wooden door. It *was* breathing. Heavy breathing. Then a kind of low moaning.

"Christ," he whispered. "He's reliving the event. They're pounding him to the cross. Oh, can't you just see it?"

Then we heard, *"Yes . . . sweet Jesus, yes."*

"But it sounds like Mama," I protested.

That's when Sammy slapped me hard against my backside and began rolling over on the linoleum floor in laughter.

"You gullible queer," he cried.

He jumped up onto the bed, holding his groin.

"I'm the Circus Man!"

In a way Sammy was. He never rode elephants or went up on the trapeze. I don't know that he ever was a barker on the midway or stuck his head into a lion's maw. But he liked to play with fire.

When I took communion for the first time—I had to learn the Twenty-third Psalm—Sammy showed up wearing Father's shoes. Mother and I sat in the car, waiting for my brother to finish dressing. She was drumming on the horn to get him moving. When she heard the backdoor slam, she shoved her foot onto the ignition and throttled our old Dodge alive, never paying him any mind.

He looked fine, dressed in his Sunday best, but then there were these several-sizes-too-large two-tone black and white dancing shoes Father donned on summer evenings when he went out alone. Sammy had stuffed newspapers into the toe boxes and wore a solemn expression.

Anxious if I'd remember the Psalm, Mother handed off the bouquet of lilacs she'd freshly cut to present to me at the close of the communion.

"Sammy, go hand these flowers to your good brother."

When he stepped into the aisle, she saw.

Parishioners cupped their hands over their mouths.

"Here, queer," he announced, awkwardly climbing the pulpit steps. "Compliments of the Circus Man."

Lying alongside him that night, "What's it feel like?" I asked, feeling the heat coming off his red backside and knowing he was hurting.

"Circus Men don't cry," he sniffed. "This ain't nothin'."

We knew it wasn't—for each of us could feel it in our bones that one day we'd hear *real breathing* outside our door.

Mother said it was going to be for Sammy or Father.

That's why he called me a queer. Father didn't, for which I was grateful.

Edward Tinsley was one, a classmate who lived two streets over who practiced the piano for three hours every day after school. He would play the *"William Tell Overture."*

"Tom, that's the shit you are going to have to listen to in heaven," Sammy said.

We preferred a blues station out of New Orleans we picked up on our portable radio after midnight on Friday evenings. Sammy said the words *jelly rolls*, *mailboxes*, and stuff like that were actually code words meaning something different.

"Howdaya know?" I asked.

"You got to have a dirty mind," he said. "Mama's 'n' yours is clean as the virgin snow—and just as cold."

Then he'd snicker, keeping time under the covers while calling out the progression of the eight-bar chords to our cracked ceiling.

Father's irreverence was more subtle.

Draping his tie over the crucifix that hung above their nuptial bed, for instance.

Or secreting spare bills he was saving for a rainy day between the pages of the Book of Revelations.

One reason for his apostasy was that our Uncle Alexander, his brother, was a Monsignor. It'd be like Sammy wearing the clown shoes, I thought.

"Tom, suppose you saw your brother dressed up in a chasuble with a big silver crucifix dangling from his neck and blowing incense out of a lantern over the parishioners' heads?"

"I'd think he was in the carnival," I said.

"Not your grandmother. She believes he's her ticket to Heaven. *'He's going to save us all . . . even if the rest of you heathens don't deserve it!'* she'd scold.

"But Alexander was a snotty-nosed prick. And now he's even a bigger one in the Roman Catholic Church.

"But don't let me stain your mind, Son. Maybe your mama is right."

I'd no sign that she was. Except my conscience talked like she was its ventriloquist.

Until the day Sammy caught farmer Eli McKinley's alfalfa field on fire. Racing through it—flames curling off him like ribbon. A charred scar in his wake. And a woman in a nearby farmhouse screaming on her porch and deranged, fanning the wind.

Father's car down by the roadside, smoke puffing from under the hood. An air filter lying on the gravel alongside Sammy's lit cigarette—and a container of gasoline.

That's when I thought that the Circus Man had finally come.

"Pay up, Sammy. Show's over."

For months Mother, Pap, and I sat next to his hospital bed listening to his labored breathing, his legs and arms suspended from some trapeze-like contraptions, and us barely able to see through the bandage mask he wore. Except his eyes still kindled.

I was grateful for that.

Because I was a pansy. Not a queer—but a pansy. I ached to be fearless like Sammy but was afraid of Heaven, the scolds who professed they were happy because they were Chosen, but I knew they could never be lighthearted like Sammy and our old man.

Theirs was a kind of brittle rapture. If you'd promise me God wouldn't seek to avenge the irreverence, I thought the joke was on them.

Except the fire queered Sammy.

He wasn't entertaining any longer. Our old man began going to bed when Mother read the Bible. He no longer smoked in bed.

Sammy even said it was time to be moving on.

"Whadaya mean?" I asked.

"Gettin' out of here."

"What about me?" I hollered.

He rolled over without answering. The next morning I awoke to find his side of the bed empty.

The only person who didn't act surprised was Father.

"Where do you think he went?" I asked.

Sammy never let on. Even to him whom I know he revered. "Papa taught us to heavy breathe," he said.

At night I'd call out, *Is that you, Circus Man? Will you give me a sign?*

But it was still as sin outside our bedroom door. Only the silver light of the moon puddling the hallway floor.

Until the day a woman phoned. "Is this Tom Wheeler?"

I said it was.

"I'm calling for Sammy," she said.

"Where is he?" I cried.

"He'd like to see you," she said softly.

A lone chapel sat at the end of winding road through a stand of pine trees. The kind you see in storybooks. I opened the doors, and there at the end of aisle under the rood was Sammy. A halo of yellow irises about his bier and clutched between his hands like a cross . . . a framing hammer.

His hands bore the white scars from the boyhood immolation. His stick legs were secreted under the satin quilt.

I'd no idea whose shoes he wore.

And he assumed this blissful expression as if he were about to share an off-color story with me.

"He talked about you quite a bit, Tom," the voice behind me said.

A comely woman with brunette hair pulled severely off her face that was shadowed by a veil dropped from a slight chapeau. I could see how Sammy would be mighty attracted to her.

"He always wanted to get back to you," she said. "'Got to see Tom, my brother. Sure miss my brother. You ought to meet him, Grace. You sure would love him. You, too, Ethan.'"

Behind her, slouched down in a pew in the dark interior of the chapel, a young boy about the age of Sammy when he first heard the Circus Man.

Ethan looked the spitting image of his dad.

"Oh, Jesus, Grace. Why'd he go?" I asked.

"Ethan says he wanted to raise some hell in heaven." She grinned.

"Maybe it's the truth," I said.

"What are you going to do?" she asked.

I couldn't answer. So many things I wanted to tell him. That our parents were both gone. And Pap's tie hanging off the crucifix was gathering dust.

That it wasn't fun any longer around the old homestead. That he had to come home. Come home to rout out the darkness, put some light back in it.

Even if it was orange.

I put my ear to his lips.

Sammy, I wanted to ask you about the note Mother had left.

Do you think she put on an act, too?

That's what I wanted to ask you, Sammy.

Which one of us did she transgress?

Me, because I was the queer? Wanting to accompany her to heaven but lusting after Pap's dancing ladies?

Was it you she transgressed, condemning you to perdition along with Father? He who embraced her china-white body while the cigarettes on the Bible waited for later. Her cold hands gripping the bed rails as he tried to push her to heaven.

And the Circus Man outside our door, shuddering, breathing hot breath like fire.

A prelude, dear Brother, to your journey across a meadow just this side of the magnolia trees, just this side of Hell.

I try to make sense of it all.
I try to put my house in order.
I try to make amends to those I've transgressed.
Some are no longer here to listen. That hurts.
And those who are . . . my words offer scarce comfort. Perhaps it's better not to say anything at all.

I THINK JESUS IS FRED ASTAIRE

Yesterday I went looking for him in Texas.

West on Route 44 then Business 77 into Kingsville. I stopped at the King Ranch museum that featured a champagne, custom-built Buick convertible with horn-back alligator seats and rifle holders in its front wheel wells. The King Saddle Shop, at the corner of Main Street, stocked fine leather valises, briefcases for folks, spatulas, and barbecue implements, club sofas and chairs, and highball glass sweat guards. A pair of red-white-and-blue women's riding boots sat in the entryway.

Outside the temperature was a sultry 103 degrees. Several parked cars, all with Texas license plates, headed into mostly vacant storefronts and pasty mannequins outfitted in LBJ-era sun-bleached attire. Underfoot, tufted carpeting mimed parched grass. A milk glass Rialto marquee advertised used radios and televisions. While inside the sole pharmacy, antique pedal cars lined a raked runway near its ceiling: a Black Maria, a WWII Army ambulance, a chrome two-seater Packard limousine with a pair of rubber ball *Oogah!* horns, and a canary yellow Hudson Terraplane.

At the apothecary's vintage soda fountain—complete with swivel-top counter seats—a Mexican waitress in a crisp white collar and bib apron asked if she could be of help.

"I'm looking for my father," I said.

"Across the street *maybe?*"

Steer horns framed the saloon's mirror and a grim-faced couple sipping margaritas from glass cactus trees. Deep in the cavernous space, fluorescent tubes illuminated a salad bar of wilted lettuce rippling under a ceiling fan.

He wasn't there either.

In fact, he'd never been farther south than Steubenville, Ohio. Perhaps he'd holed up in a rundown bungalow along Main Street, reclining on a swayback bunk, his undershirt and briefs wicking sweat, laughing to himself, wondering how in God's name he ended up in the southern panhandle—Kingsville no less.

At five o'clock he'd wander up Main Street to peer into the Saddle Shop's windows, recalling the life he once aspired to. Or pay the museum token to stare at the customized motorcar that exhaled Texas aristocracy and untold wealth . . . picturing himself slumped in its backseat, a highball in hand, a long-legged Texan beauty alongside.

He never gave a damn about guns; rustling steers didn't particularly excite him either. Hard drinking women who dressed like flowers that floated in gin drinks did. Their bluebonnet scent and Indian-blanket *patois* . . . an antidote to prairie dust and drought, stained mattress ticking, and termites chewing away at the sills underneath. Their wispy laughter a palliative to the defunct Frigidaire's lukewarm beer, and two eggs fried in a black skillet over a hot plate.

King Saddle Shop was the *dream replenisher*, the confirmation that he hadn't been living a lie. That, in fact, the three-story stucco mansions had Spanish tile floors, cool shuttered interiors, four poster beds dressed in Devonshire cream linens, mahogany bars stocked with crystal decanters of bourbon and gin, lemons and limes overflowing *barro negro* pottery, and highball glasses one could barely get his fist around endured.

And when he strolled at half light past the neon marquee, he saw the chiaroscuro face of Ingrid Bergman materialize on the screen inside its black interior. How moviedom had once swaddled him in air-conditioned starlets, pick of the line of ragtops, and the drama of living with a song always in one's heart—a refrain of hope to lure loss around some unintended bend where life sparkled and there were always crisp twenties in his trousers.

The movie palace was his sanctuary of classy dames whose lantern faces insinuated scarlet concupiscence. Lumière goddesses draped chaise lounges, or danced across marble stages with gentlemen shadows—the cathedral of veiled light, instructing how *he* was completed by such creatures, how little he was without one.

But there weren't any in Kingsville.

Inside its Rialto metal shelves stocked circa '60s and '70s wooden TV sets, their picture tube screens channeling snow. Molded plastic compact radios, Admirals, Crosleys, and RCAs. No soundtrack even in the place. A lone Mexican sitting alongside a cash box asked if he could be of any help.

"I'm looking for my father," I said. "Thought he might have wandered inside here."

"Been nobody in here for days, mister."

"Uh-huh. I think he's down the street a bit."

"Y'all come back," he said without a hint of irony.

In my boyhood we rode the midnight tracks of Mahoningtown, Ambridge, and Philadelphia to Grand Central Station where we'd taxi to the Waldorf. "This is where those celluloid folks live," he said. In our hometown motion pictures didn't vent fragrance. Here I could smell the stars for the first time.

The bellhop opened our door and unveiled the show, taxi horns rising up from the streets below. The room's chintz-laden interior, its hexagonal tile bathroom with a shower, silver fixtures, and towels whose heft and whiteness mocked our lavatory's dark interior and tub in which Father had to pull his knees to his chest when he bathed.

Manhattan was the Temple of America, the Rialto.

Before our junkets (we made several in my youth), he'd buy on credit the finest suit in Jack Hart's Haberdashery. "Going to the big city with my son," he'd say. "Want to look appropriate." I knew he wanted to look like Ray Milland or Cary Grant.

Once he bought a white linen suit and a straw hat with a chartreuse silk puggaree. He looked like an author, some famous philanthropist, even a gigolo out of a grade B flick. Nobody in our hometown dressed like that. Even the bankers, the judges, and the doctors didn't. "This is what they wear in the big city," the salesman said.

The Saddle Shop conserved the myth.

Near Kingsville there still were Rialto acolytes. Mexicans cleaned their domiciles, prepared their foods, and serviced their everyday needs.

He had to come here to die.

Christ, it was all so painful when I realized it. *He's down there in one of those damn shacks with the lopsided porches and sweating death.*

Waiting for me to sit across from him in the sweltering heat, the daylight turned amber through the torn window blinds, the radio playing static and some country western tune.

"You been to the Rialto?" He'd grin ruefully like it was the biggest joke ever played on anybody, let alone his only damn son.

"I didn't know. I swear to God I didn't know," raising his arms to the cracked ceiling in protest. Sure of my being about to criticize him for leading me astray.

"I'da told you, Son. Surer than Christ, I'da let you in on the secret if I'da known myself. But I was snookered, too."

He never took me to church, for which I was always grateful. Instead, we journeyed to the cinema. It's where the little backwaters of towns like ours eventually flowed. The dream lotuses of the grain fields and the burgs of smoke and ash producing commerce, their black metal cylinders and stacks silhouetting the skyline like cities of their own, but cities where nobody lived. Tube and metal skyscrapers billowing smoke, soot, and sulfur. At night strings of lights, adorning them like industrial trees. Oil-encrusted cities, dotting the skyline. Blinking red lights on their towers alerting air craft. These were the production centers of our iron-rust states that folks like my father—the dreamers of a better, more fanciful life—were escaping.

"We're going to the skyscrapers, aeries of rooms with quiet lights and thick carpets, walls of glass, women in the hallways whose dresses make subtle noises in the wind they themselves create as they pass, their fragrance lighting our minds.

"This is where we're headed, Son.

"Your mother insists Grand Central is up there somewhere," he gestured heavenward. "You can't get to it by air, boat, or train. You can only get to it on the back of Jesus. Well, let me clue you in on a secret, Son.

You can't fly if you ain't got wings.

"So you and me, we're not gonna be with Mama and all her relatives in Valhalla at picnic tables out in some cow pasture, eatin' potato salad and corn on the cob for eternity. The women in their flower-sack dresses, the men wearing braces and trousers hiked up tight to their groins. Waitin'. Waitin' for the train of glory to take them on to the mansion of Jehovah.

"My darling son . . . that train of glory ain't ever gonna whistle through the skies. D'ya know why? 'Cause a train needs *coal* to run; it needs *oil* to run. It needs *steam* to whistle . . . and that all comes from under the clay we're now standing on. Out of the hard earth, boy. Just like you 'n' me. And the train we be riding on to Glory is *goin' to the Rialto*, the big city, the cloud piercers of concrete that climb to the moon. And the women there will be real. They be breathing larkspur and primrose and hyacinth and bougainvillea through their gossamer dresses, and we can see their clean feet tramping down the carpeted hallways—they be coming to meet us. And these peaches, boy, don't eat potato salad and read the scripture while they're waitin' for the glory train; they be singing how they need men and boys, how we be laying alongside them and making dreams together, how we be dancing with them way up in our aeries where there is no soot outside the glass, no stench of sulfur, no black tankers of industry squatting like vultures on the horizon—just linen suits, boy, white linen dresses, creamy shoes, and lipstick and blush the shade of lust.

"That's where the train of glory is headed.

"Women like your mama keep their legs closed for Jesus. We're goin' where they drink champagne instead of root beer. Where the opposite sex look like tall glasses of gin and tonic instead of sarsaparilla.

"Furthermore, I think Jesus is Fred Astaire."

And he laughed, just up the street from the pharmacy where the kiddie cars rode high on its walls, the saloon with no patrons, and one block away from the only picture show in town—the Saddle Shop. And the museum closes on Saturday at four. The dead battery in the bubbly Buick convertible with its mellifluous horn prods the St. Gerstein heifers—dusty as the Texan earth—aside, crystal decanters of bourbon compartmented in its backseat.

Kingsville . . . the cemetery of the Rialto.

Father waiting for me to return to the place we'd never been.

Christ, I wanted to dance with the master as he did. I wanted to make love to Ingrid Bergman like Bogie did. I wanted to always have my hair slicked back, and reside in black-and-white rooms with monochrome skies like the celluloid people did, too. For they never sweated in their aeries. It was always cool there. Cool like dreams. The color of red, cerise, mustard yellow, or indigo blue never gave shade to the chiaroscuro melancholia that I suffer now.

I heard him cry for me. Standing in boxer shorts and undershirt, the perspiration dripping off a three-day stubble, "Come back, Son," he moaned. "Jesus Christ, come back. I can't go to the Rialto alone."

I know what he meant.

How can you stand in front of the Saddle Shop, your nose pressed to its dark lantern interior, the salespersons dressed in crisp white linen suits, its hide couches and sofa squeaking of deep wealth . . . and dream, if you are standing outside and the pavement is 110 degrees?

And the saloon down the street is the appointed front with nothing inside—a movie set on the Train Bound for Glory Line.

ST. JAMES HOTEL

Yet another elegant hotel in a strange town.

I'd meet her in the Basilica-hush lobby, we'd have drinks alongside a grand piano that played itself, then ride the gilded cage to our room . . . always with a northern view. This one happened to look out upon a shipping channel where oil freighters passed at night, skyscrapers slinking outside our window.

These were clandestine rendezvous except her other self knew perfectly well I was cheating on her.

Our children were grown. We'd had a trusting marriage and lovely house with terra cotta planters whose pansies cascaded its stoop—a halcyon time in our lives, only we shared a dark premonition that we were sliding inexorably into the sea.

At night we were lulled to sleep by waves washing stones back and forth on the ocean's edge. The sound of bowling balls ceaselessly tossed by citizen ghosts, their convening at dusk a short stroll from the cemetery off the village green. On the beach lay remnants of a capacious mansion's stone foundation. Its rooms long since slipped out to the deep. Some days the cellar walls rose out of the sand as if to reclaim its site; mostly they lay buried, leaving no trace.

But Alba and I knew what once stood there.

The house had a veranda and a Queen Anne tower with convex windows. It's red slate tile roof at sunset glistening with sea vapor . . . bougainvillea, japonica, mimosa, hibiscus skirting its foundation.

"It's too close to the water," Alba said. "It's only half awake."

To her that meant the mansion was straddling a dream. Its stone and tile reality barely a step off its veranda to the waterline. And the nightly bowlers.

"Like you and me, Daniel. Our house, too, is slipping off."

But we were a street away.

Alba would walk to the old Rose foundation at night and stand where the living room once stood. From a discreet distance I'd watch as she separated the drapes and gazed in her summer linens at the horizon line. Kelp-brown hair looping off her narrow shoulders, her pallor white as the surf, the mist of her breath clouding and un-clouding the window. A photograph in glass.

Soon I, too, began to share her dream . . . or so it seemed.

Did she see herself as the lost Mrs. Rose? For whom was she watching? Mr. Rose had owned a tanning factory in the nearby industrial town where he spent his waking hours. Townsfolk recall the childless couple sitting on the verandah of a Sunday afternoon. Mrs. Rose, "stately as her shingled cottage" the old-timers said, seldom ventured out in the sun and was always dressed in white. He in a rumpled black suit. "A businessman type," they characterized him, "balding, a bit curt when spoken to, but proud of what he owned: Mrs. Rose and their dwelling by the sea."

One November morning a Northeastern storm destroyed the residence. First the great verandah was separated from the body of the house. Its wicker chaise lounges, rockers and chairs flew down the coastline like geese. Onlookers swore Mrs. Rose stood unperturbed in the tower window, watching the event unfold. Then the north side of the house was peeled away, including Mr. Rose's garage housing their Packard. The sedan sank backwards into the slurry, its silver grill lingering as if uttering a mute shriek.

Still Mrs. Rose stood steadfast. But unlike the rest of the mansion, the tower serenely rolled over on its side as the beach eroded about it, and in minutes, submerged—the lady supine against the wall opposite the window, no longer staring at the raging sea... but through her sepulcher's porthole to the darkening sky.

Then gone.

The bowling balls furiously in play.

• • •

I never let on to Alba that I was a witness to her evening beach strolls.

At night as I lay alongside her, not certain if she was asleep or awake, the bowlers—their fury became more pronounced. They were rolling closer to our house.

Alba didn't stir.

Nor did she stir when the shutters banged against the shingles. The window panes rattled in their sashes. Cupboard, closet, and empty bedroom doors banged open and shut as fickle drafts strolled our hallways.

I pictured her standing in the Rose tower, waiting.

One night when the bowling balls were feverishly cavorting the coastline, I sat up on one elbow and looked down at her. She lay with her eyes wide open staring at the pine tree, its moonlit shadows, sweeping across our ceiling. Like dark sands migrating across our bodies. It cast a hypnotic effect on her.

"Alba?"

"Better put the car in the garage," she said.

But we owned no car.

"The wicker furniture—it's time to bring it in for the winter, Daniel."

"The planters of bougainvillea?" I asked.

"Yes, those, too."

"But it's only September," I said.

"The bowlers are migrating here by the hundreds. Can't you hear?"

She was impatient.

"Yes," I said. "Tomorrow, Alba, tomorrow, I'll begin winterizing the house."

She sighed as if relieved.

"Go to sleep, dearest," I urged. "The sky will be gloriously clear tomorrow. The bougainvillea hasn't dropped its petals yet. The sounds we hear this evening are merely your memories.

"I'll see you in the morning."

When she awoke, she set about her daily chores. For all the years we lived in the house, our furniture was never rearranged. The many paintings and photographs on the walls and surfaces throughout the house . . . those, too, remained fixed. "It's where they always belong," Alba would say. So, too, indigo-blue bath towels draped from glass tubes. The precise manner in which the beds were made—feather pillows fluffed then dressed, depending on the season, by shams coordinated with the bedspreads. Window shades raised to the third sash mullion each daybreak.

And in our pantry, gleaming from behind glass cabinets, gold-edged china for company that seldom came, and a set of Fiestaware for us.

But this daybreak she discovered a vellum envelope on her kitchen chair, her name in ink script across its sealed surface.

It wasn't in my handwriting.

"Dearest Alba,

"Kindly dress in your summer whites, that pleated linen skirt and blouse with the collar and bone-buttoned front . . . open at the neck so that I might see the garnet necklace. And those white heels with the single strap and your silk hose, the shade of dune grass, please, Alba wear these when we meet at the St. James. I've enclosed a ticket. You mustn't tell anybody.

"With love.

"A Stranger."

The following week she ceased her nightly walks. One sundown I caught her sitting in bed with a towel under her feet, her skirt hiked above her knees, applying a vermillion polish to her toenails.

They'd always been clear—like the backs of crabs.

"How lovely," I said.

"Oh," she explained. "A hoarfrost this morning. I'm doing something silly to cheer myself up."

Then I noticed packages from local stores multiplying about the house. Undergarments from the lingerie boutique. Lovely tortoise shell clips for her hair, a pair of leather strap-sandals with open toes secreted in the bottom of her closet.

Upon entering the bedroom one evening, I was overcome by the potent scent of perfume or cologne. Our house was unused to affected odors except, perhaps, the curious aroma of an over-worked vacuum machine.

In bed Alba smelled like saltwater spray.

"Winter's coming," she calmly announced on the eve of her departure. "I won't be able to visit my sister when the snow flies. She's invited me up for a couple days. You don't mind do you, Daniel?"

At some level she must have realized that I, too, welcomed the opportunity to get away from her. Always loath to blame others for any problems she might be suffering, "Oh it's just as much my do-ings as it is theirs," her common refrain.

"There's plenty of food for you here in the pantry, Daniel."

"Treat yourself to a lovely flowered dress," I said, slipping money into her purse.

"Let Elise know how wonderful summer's been here on the coast. Encourage her to visit us one day so that you and she can take daily strolls to the beach.

"You go there too often alone," I said, staring at her.

She registered no surprise.

At sunup, ravishing in a pearl linen pleated skirt and matching sleeveless blouse, the secreted sandals, and her hair in a single braid that swept the small of her back, she walked out our path. It was as if the memory of Mrs. Rose and the foundation had vanished. Only faint sounds of the stone bowlers miles up the waterfront.

"Goodbye, dearest," I said.

"Goodbye, Daniel."
Who was she seeing?

The previous night, I'd sensed a much younger, more vibrant, Alba, lying alongside me. She had bathed in a brilliant purple cologne and her hair had been subtly oiled; from it rose a strong fragrance. Outside the Rose mansion through lilac foliage I saw the ashen figure of Mrs. Rose looking out to sea.

I presume most men could imagine nothing more painful than being cuckolded. Death, the prospect of facing it unexpectedly, didn't engage me as much. To consider, however, that another suitor would lie alongside my white-limbed Alba, and, intoxicated by the scent of sea anemones rising off her breasts, spread himself over her as if he were shadowing her from a hot afternoon sun . . .

Made me want to cry out. To begin heaving my chest, shrieking, howling up and down the barren shore for the man—the bowler— who had come to take her away.

And then I thought . . . *Is this what Mrs. Rose had waited for?*

Had one roused from his diurnal chore of mocking time by rolling the stone up and back again . . . and spied her in the round tower window?

She beckoning he visit her upstairs to give her a taste of winter.

The bougainvillea had turned too sweet.

The lilac too fragrant.

Mr. Rose—he kept returning home bearing flowers.

• • •

So I meet Alba at the St. James.

It's how we ward off death.

We become unfaithful to each other.

Our room overlooks the Notre Dame Basilica with its twin towers of Temperance and Perseverence. Inside one is a many ton bell that rings across this city of one hundred carillons. The other houses seven thousand pipes to the electro-pneumatic organ that sits in the baptistry.

Alba asks me to make love to her in such a way that I might erase her guilt of leaving me back home one street away from the mansion that slid out to sea.

"Make me forget, Daniel," she whispers.

"That sun over time fades vermillion.

"That winter gives rise to infidelity."

She opens to me like the sea, pulling me into her, uttering sounds that I occasionally heard emanating from the Rose foundation . . . as if somebody were alive in those invisible rooms, calling to themselves while scurrying through its paneled hallways.

"Don't tell, Daniel," she asks.

"Don't tell him about death. For he will be afraid. And jealous."

I didn't understand.

"Winter's coming," she repeated. "We've only so much time you and I. Let him worry about storing the wicker, trundling the plant urns to the cellar, readying the storm windows.

"But in your arms, in this room that overlooks a Basilica, the sound of time is far down the strand. Here bougainvillea never dies. The heady odor of French lilac is the scent of a harlot.

"I, Mrs. Rose.

"My men all return. Yet they are strangers to each other.

"They roll stones up and down the coastline at night, awaiting my visit.

"But tonight you're mine."

BIOGRAPHICAL NOTE

Dennis Must is the author of two short story collections: *Oh, Don't Ask Why* (Red Hen Press, 2007) and *Banjo Grease* (Creative Arts Book Company, 2000). His plays have been performed Off-Off-Broadway, and his fiction has appeared in numerous anthologies and literary journals. He has worked as a cabinet-maker, short-order cook, lightning rod installer, florist, bartender, bellhop, and as a general laborer in a glass factory, steel mill, on highway construction, and on the Baltimore & Ohio Railroad. For over a decade, he was Executive Vice President of Corporate Space, Inc., a commercial real estate firm in Boston he co-founded. He lives in Salem, Massachusetts.

CPSIA information can be obtained
at www.ICGtesting.com
Printed in the USA
LVHW040201161022
730794LV00001B/108

9 781597 090339